WILDERNESS
UNTAMED

WILDERNESS UNTAMED

SA KANDASAMY
Translated by Vasantha Surya

Published by
Renu Kaul Verma
Vitasta Publishing Pvt Ltd
4348/4C, Ansari Road, Daryaganj
New Delhi - 110 002
info@vitastapublishing.com

ISBN 978-81-19670-54-3

Original in Tamil, *Saaya Vanam*, © SA Kandasamy, 1968

First published in English, *The Defiant Jungle* © Vasantha Surya, INDIAN WRITING, 2009

Wilderness Untamed © Vasantha Surya
First Edition 2025

The contents of the book reflect the views of the author and translator. The Tamil Nadu Textbook and Educational Services Corporation is not responsible for the same.

This is a work of fiction and all characters and incidents described in this book are the product of the authors' imagination. Any resemblance to actual persons, living or dead, is entirely coincidental.

All rights reserved. No part of this publication may be reproduced, stored in a retrieval system, or transmitted, in any form or by any means, electronic, mechanical, photocopying, recording or otherwise, without the prior permission of the publishers. The publisher is in no way responsible for the opinions expressed in this book.

Cover & Layout by Somesh Kumar Mishra
Printed by Chaman Enterprises, Delhi

TRANSLATION INITIATIVE OF THE TAMIL NADU TEXTBOOK AND EDUCATIONAL SERVICES CORPORATION

This is an initiative of the Tamil Nadu Textbook and Educational Services Corporation (TNTB & ESC) under the aegis of one of the announcements for the year 2021-22, by Honourable Minister for School Education Thiru. Anbil Mahesh Poyyamozhi to identify and translate into English, Kannada, Malayalam and Telugu, Tamil literary works, that they might enhance the reach of Tamil antiquity, tradition and contemporaneity and enrich world literature and to also translate significant literary voices from other Dravidian languages into Tamil. Both ventures are to be undertaken as either independent or joint publications with collaborating publishers.

Members, Academic Advising Committee (Translation)
Dr. R. Balakrishnan, IAS, Researcher and Writer
Thiru. S. Ramakrishnan, Writer
Thiru. S. Madasamy, Educationist

Project Execution Team
Thiru. Dindigul I. Leoni, Chairperson, TNTB & ESC
Tmt. R. Gajalakshmi, IAS, Managing Director, TNTB & ESC
Dr. S. Kannappan, Member Secretary, TNTB & ESC
Thiru. R. Dhayalan, Financial Advisor, TNTB & ESC
Dr. T. S. Saravanan, Joint Director (Translations), TNTB & ESC
Thiru. P. A. Arumugam, Deputy Director (Publications), TNTB & ESC
Dr. P. Saravanan, Assistant Director (Publications), TNTB & ESC
Thiru. M. Appanasamy, Consultant, TNTB & ESC
Tmt. Mini Krishnan, Co-ordinating Editor, TNTB & ESC

UNEARTHING AMBIGUITIES
A Translator's Introduction

> '...the appetite for conquest bumps into
> walls that defy its assault...'
> – Albert Camus

Like Sisyphus who tried to climb a mountain and found himself endlessly staving off a boulder that was hurtling upon him, humankind is constantly grappling with the fact that the summit of 'progress' is out of sight. The way ahead is fraught with dangers, few of them foreseen. The ground under the feet cannot be taken for granted.

The 1960s were a time when orators-turned-writers were vying to be heard as liberators of the Tamil language. A notable deviation from the first exuberant waves of this Tamil post-colonial current was the unpretentious intensity of Sa Kandasamy's first novel, **Saaya Vanam**, published in 1969. In the dispassionate tone which has established him as a reliable literary witness, Kandasamy tells the story of how a South Indian forest rich in honey and tamarind is destroyed to make way for sugarcane plantations and a sugar mill. Because it evokes the ambiguities unearthed when man reshapes the natural environment, this novel has a deserved place in the world literature of globalization.

It describes an entire eco-system, inclusive of its human element, in textured detail and lays bare the mixed motives of those who mount an audacious assault on it.

A simple fact has ensured the dominant position of sugarcane as a food crop: this plant happens to be the most efficient converter of the sun's energy into calories for human consumption. 'Sugar has arguably had as great an impact on the environment as any other agricultural commodity,' according to a report in the World Wildlife Fund magazine (2015) entitled **Sugarcane Farming's Toll on the Environment,** with the telling sub-title 'Bitter Price'.

It happened in living memory in Kandasamy's homeland, the Kaveri delta. When sugarcane from the West Indies entered India as a plantation crop capable of enormous yields but demanding new methods and intensive inputs (unlike the traditional 'thin' sugarcane of India), the decadent mirasidari system began to topple. Interlocking caste and kinship hierarchies based on rigid patriarchy had established themselves here over centuries. Customary and often capricious entitlements to land and water-use, to the labour of those without land, and to the produce thus obtained, sustained this Indian avatar of feudalism. Propped up against the forested hinterland were lands on which grew dryland millets and some paddy. By the 1930's the agro-industry of sugarcane, along with wage labour and the cash economy, had transformed livelihoods and lifestyles. Agriculture now fed directly into the industrialisation process, with both water-guzzling paddy and sugarcane dictating land use. Rivers began to be harnessed for irrigation, and the terrain to be reshaped.

In ***Saaya Vanam,*** the agent of change is a man who has nothing to lose. Born to an indentured coolie mother who left her birthplace with her child for sheer survival's sake, Chidambaram returns with a little money and a little knowledge of what is going on in the world. He buys a piece of forested land and sets out to pursue his goals. Unhampered by nostalgia and fired by the entrepreneurial spirit, he is a true modern, individualistic and aspirational. Standing apart from the web of custom, he inserts into village life a catalyst of sugar, encapsulated in a new work ethic. A whole new way of doing things, it is received at first with scepticism, and is finally accepted. The idea pierces through the slowly rotting social fabric and breaks up the very contours of the land. Which meant that the forest had to go.

'…Like a lion in the first flush of its golden-maned youth, the forest of giant golden-stemmed bamboos burst from the earth and seemed to stalk towards them. How could one even dream of hewing down this awesome bamboo and dragging it away? Around each clump was a twisting braid of briars. Every thorn would have to be sliced off separately before the stalks could be cut loose…'

Frustrated in his efforts to carve his dream of sugarcane fields and a sugar mill from the entrails of the jungle, Chidambaram hits upon the age-old solution:

'Why not burn all this? Green shoots and all?'

The jungle does not take kindly to this assault. In his introduction to the twelfth edition (2022) of Kandasamy's Tamil original, Paavannan speaks of how Chidambaram is diminished as a human being by his success in clearing it. And because he has managed to share his dream with others, flames soon consume not only the bamboos but the entire forest, with all its animals and birds. A pair of squirrels are charred to death, casting a seed of sour self-doubt into his consciousness.

It is no small matter to clear a jungle, and over time, humankind has been just too successful at it. For as long as we can remember, this has been the stuff of heroic legend, as in the Mahabharata when Arjuna and Krishna burned down the Khandava forest to create pastures for cattle and fields for crops. In the anecdotes that Kandasamy puts in the mouths of the characters, particularly the redoubtable Sivanaandi Thevar, there is a wondering sense of the absurd. We discern a tenderness not only towards the mortally wounded jungle, but also towards people 'who know not what they do'.

Kandasamy comes out with an occasional treat for the translator – a prophetic voice, as in the very first chapter:

'**...the whole forest would reverberate with the**

sounds of the tamarind being harvested, every branch and stem of the trees shuddering as though buffeted by the oozhi-kaatru…'

The oozhi-kaatru is the maelstrom at aeon's end. This whirlwind at the end of the Kali-Yuga ushers in another revolution of the endlessly whirling wheel of Time, a metaphor intrinsic to the idiom of Tamil. Permeated as it is with the cosmology of the Saiva, Shakta, and Vaishnava traditions, it is rooted in a primeval insight with a universal resonance: that this earth is not an *akshayapatra*, an inexhaustible cornucopia.

'Somebody will have to write a new Mahabharata of our blind kings acquiescing in the conversion of this once fertile country into a vast wasteland,' wrote Shailendra Nath Ghosh, one of the country's earliest environmentalists and a social philosopher. He pointed out that 'soils planted with water-intensive crops march towards ruination', that large landholders are growing cash crops unsuited to their soils, and warned that the much-touted grandiose scheme of linking India's rivers, if ever realized, will be a 'disaster'. (*The Millennial Folly,* 2003*).* In her passionate 'Republic of Dreams' speech at the Frankfurt Book Fair in 2006, the writer Mahasweta Devi declared, 'I wish for the environment to be protected, to be loved and restored. I wish the land to be healed, the waters to be pure again. For the tiger to survive.' Over the last fifty years, through the 'tree-hugging' Chipko and Narmada Andolan movements and dozens of other protests, including the latest on June 25, 2024 in Dehra Dun against the felling of trees, the concept of 'sustainability' has trickled into the consciousness of millions. The hubris of 'progress' is being viewed askance as a freebie drug, in lieu of sustainable development.

Today it is clear that the vital environmental context, with its endlessly sprouting questions, cannot be left to academics and journalists alone. The literary imagination must explore and address it. Kandasamy's is one such vision, and one such voice. Written when Sa Kandasamy was just twenty-five years old, **Saaya Vanam** brings the jungle alive, along with those who try to destroy it. The theme – development versus environment – was not exactly politically correct in 1969, but emerges as nothing short of prescient, fifty-five years later. It is slowly dawning on us that environmental concerns are far from irrelevant to here-and-now human needs and aspirations.

Yet there is nothing polemical at all about **Saaya Vanam**. It is a piece of controlled articulation with vital silences suspended between the words. For the meaning to swim from Tamil into English, and not merely survive but also thrive, the translator must carry across these elisions like oxygen-bearing air bubbles, without breaking too many. The frequent slurring and muting that cushion his words recall the phonetic contractions and omissions typical of Tamil. For comprehension, these elisions require each string of syllables to be mentally unwound, and in translation they require careful transfer to another 'word-spool'. Because Kandasamy's Tamil never gets unravelled from the central spool of what he wants to convey, and because he never lets words get entangled in irrelevant knots, translating his work has been a deeply satisfying experience. His **Saaya Vanam** emboldened me to translate other contemporary writers who evoke that sensibility, Cho Dharman and Imayam among them.

Of the linguistic environment, we are also growing increasingly aware. Intertwining branches of translation keep sprouting from the innumerable trees of human speech. In the first introduction (2009) to **The Defiant Jungle**, I wrote: 'I have not been searching for correspondences or striving for fidelity so much as trying to open portals through today's English (including Indian English) into the world of Kandasamy's Tamil novel. A translation which is so 'smooth' that the reader forgets he or she is reading a translation is, to my mind, a failure. I wanted readers to remain constantly aware as they turned each page that they were listening to people who speak and think in Tamil, who live and work in that particular part of Tamil Nadu. The awareness of the stubborn walls in which these portals are set promotes a kind of tension, a Brechtian alienation that enhances the overall literary experience. Hence certain Tamil names, words and terms serve as entry points, and need to stand out and be counted as such in their original forms, not just for the sake of accuracy but in fact because they enrich English, the language of translation.'

Tamil literature has from the earliest times been infused with the awareness of the land, as the 'thinai' concept in Sangam poetry shows. The almost tangible sense of the sights, sounds, and smells of the Tamil country in this novel reminds us that Tamil itself – like any human speech – is an outgrowth of the natural world. Kandasamy's novel about the lush Kaveri delta flows naturally, along with references to many plants and trees. Some plant products are consumed as food, and some have medicinal uses. The very first sentence in the novel speaks of the 'puliyanthope' – meaning 'tamarind grove'. The Tamil word 'puli' is a household word, the distinctive flavour of the region's cuisine. It comes from the tamarind's sour taste... actually slightly sweet, which explains why the Arabic-speaking merchants who came across it in India likened it to dates – 'tamar-e-hind' meaning 'date of India'.

I have in most instances used both Tamil and their equivalents in English in my rendering, adjusting their placement and inserting words and phrases to enable the reader to visualise them without the narrative losing its tempo. These and other Tamil words have been retained because they are part of Indian English ('Tamlish') speech. The work of two remarkable linguists, Rama Kant Agnihotri and G.N.Devy, has confirmed some of my gut feelings about language in this country. Today speakers and readers of every language – English included – are listening to words that are new, and which quickly grow on them. For instance, has it been possible – or even necessary – to find 'pure' yet usable 'shudh Hindi', or Tamil terms for 'bus' and 'phone', and now for 'internet' and 'email'?

Sa Kandasamy is not with us today to see his ***Saaya Vanam***'s English avataar being reborn. I am grateful that he gave me free rein to render this work in English (as he did his ***Visaaranai Commission – The Enquiry Commission***) as I saw fit. Both he and Rohini Kandasamy generously gave of their time, clearing doubts and providing background perspectives. Of great help in finding equivalents for some names of plants, trees, fish, etc. were A.V. Balasubramanian and his colleagues at the Centre for Indian Knowledge Systems, Chennai, and S. Ramakrishnan and D. Asaithambi of ***Mozhi***. A walk in the Guindy Reserve Forest in the company of the forest ranger, Shri Murugaraj, and a visit to the Centre for Ecological Sciences at the Indian Institute of Science in Bangalore helped me visualize the actual shapes and colours of the ***Saaya Vanam***.

Under its new title, ***Wilderness Untamed***, in this updated edition being brought out by Vitasta, has now been included in the Tamil Nadu Textbook and Educational Services Corporation's scheme of enabling translations and re-publishing already translated works of note for the benefit of college and school students, as well as for the general reader. 'Spreading literature beyond linguistic barriers' is the goal of the TNTBESC, in the words of T.S.Saravanan, Deputy Director (Translations). Mini Krishnan, Coordinating Editor, who has helped birth many translations in this multi-lingual country, has brought to this project her editorial acumen and her wide-ranging knowledge of India's literatures. I have benefited greatly, as a translator and as a friend, from her listening ear.

Vasantha Surya

Chapter 01

PAUSING AT THE edge of the dark dense puliyanthope, Chidambaram looked up at the sky. A flock of pond herons swooped low and flew by, followed by cranes, their necks outstretched. Then a single crow pheasant, and two flocks of green parakeets.

Presently, the sky cleared.

Parting the straggling branches of honeythorn shrubs and scratched by the burrs of the prickly chaff, he reached a narrow track in the underbrush. A path about a foot wide had been pressed into the earth by the herdsboys' feet as they followed their foraging cattle through the tamarind grove into the wilderness. This meandering trail changed with the seasons, stretching and shrinking, and sometimes going off by itself to peter out entirely.

Such jungle paths are usually short-distance trails. They twist and turn but don't last long, shaped as they are by the weather and the whims of young cowherds. Each trail is within calling distance of another such, but they don't merge with one another to form broader trails that might cover longer distances. One such trail stretched from the main road to the tree with the parrot-beak mangoes. Another led from the banyan to the 'sleepyface' raintree by the Muneeswaran shrine, whose leaves drooped shut at dusk. A third went from the iluppai to the guava.

Beyond, there were no tracks. No sign at all of men having cut a path through the jungle. If you ever had to go in there, you would have to beat your way through the dense nochi and the thorny kaarai, trampling and crushing the grassblades underfoot.

Nobody really knew very much about the trees, bushes and creepers that girdled and bound this untamed wilderness on all sides. Not one person had ever gone in there and come back whole.

One afternoon, nine years ago, Karuppanna Thevar had gone some distance into the Saaya Vanam in search of a wayward cow, when something blurred the way ahead and he stumbled back, blood spurting from his mouth. And died, three days later.

The villagers' forays into the forest mostly came to an end after this. Nobody ventured beyond the tamarinds. The jungle seemed to have drawn a line right there. A veritable boundary, you might say. Saaya Vanam – 'The Forest that would not be Felled' – on whose fringes stood the dark, dense tamarind grove.

The village, too, bore the same name.

When the tamarind trees began to drop their ripened fruit, the cowherds would go and inform Sivanandi Thevar, who would wait another five-six days, then go and take a look all by himself. Seizing the lowest branch, he would give it a good shake and bring the dark reddish-black pods rattling down, to be trapped on the branches of the nochi and the kaarai shrubs. Picking them out carefully, and leaving them in a heap under the tree, he would return with an army of labourers trooping behind him. The forest would then echo with the sounds of the tamarind being harvested, every bough and twig shuddering helplessly as though buffeted by the oozhi kaatru itself, the whirlwind that ushers in an aeon's end.

There was an order in the way Thevar harvested the tamarind. He always began at the southern end and proceeded in a southeasterly direction right up to the northern corner. If you asked him why, he couldn't have told you. That was the path taken by his father and his grandfather, and those before them, and all he did was to follow it without deviating in the slightest.

Every household got their year's supply of puli from a particular tree. The pods of the sweet tamarind in the southern part of the grove went to Sambamurthi Iyer's house. Those from the short tree went to the Peria Pannai, the biggest landlord of those parts. The tamarind from the southeastern tree near the Kathavarayan shrine was meant for Patanjali Shastri's household, and the tall tree's pods for Parthasarathi Iyengar. Every single tree was separately shaken down; the pods of one never got mixed up with the pods of another. He saw to all that, working calmly and steadily amid all that hectic noise and activity. For about seven or eight days, while the first crop was being shaken down, the grove would hum with all the comings and goings. Then it would sink back into profound silence, until the pods began to fall once again.

Chidambaram leaned against a solitary toddy-palm on the bank of the Vettaru, the stream that had cut its way through the wilderness, and gazed into the distance. Hearing a jangling of bells, he narrowed his eyes and craned forward. There was no sign of bullocks. None of a cart either. But the bells grew louder. Descending from the canal bank, he walked along tracks pressed into the mud by cartwheels and stopped under a straight-trunked punnai.

Sambamurthi Iyer got down from the covered bullock cart. He was followed by his accountant, who held on to the cart and stood a little distance away. Eagerly, Chidambaram looked to see if anyone else was with them. There was no one. It pleased him very much that Iyer had brought his accountant along. He brought his palms together in a greeting.

Throwing his angavastram over his shoulder, Iyer remarked, 'Came much earlier, did you, Chidambaram? There was something to be done on the way, Annasami turned up, and that took some time...'

'I just arrived, sir. I barely came and stood here – and you arrived.'

'Is that so!'

Tossing back a lock of hair from his brow, Chidambaram quickly ran his eyes over Iyer. Unlike himself, the man had not chosen to cut his hair short in the modern style. Smooth-shaven from forehead to crown, Iyer sported an enormous kudumi at the back of his head. As large as that impressive knot of hair was his broad, handsome, frank face. Large too, were his eyes and his ears. His diamond ear-studs, twice the size of those worn by the accountant, flashed each time he turned.

'Kadukkans look very good on you, sir!' remarked Chidambaram.

'I've worn them for as long as I can remember.'

'Oh?'

'Father wore even grander ones.'

'Mm,' murmured Chidambaram.

'So many different kinds he used to wear...'

Chidambaram wagged his head in admiration.

'Sami, sun's going down...' piped up the accountant by way of a reminder.

'Yes, yes,' nodded Iyer. He secured his veshti tightly around his waist and strode on ahead.

This was probably just the second or the third time in his whole life that Sambamurthi Iyer had set foot in this forest that he had always called his own. His amazement was boundless, and he walked on in a happy daze, greedily taking in its luxuriant foliage. He tore off a leaf from a wild castor bush, then tossed it away, drops of milky sap dripping from the stem. Then he climbed up a slope overgrown with punnai and guava all the way to the summit of a hillock, as though to survey his territory. From this point the jungle's whole expanse could not be viewed, but he could see its awesome frontage. Looping together earth and sky in skeins of green was a prodigious expanse of bush and tree and vine. Bamboos towered over the fruit-bearing tamarinds, the iluppais with their sweet-tasting flowers and their oil-yielding buttery nuts and the jack trees with gigantic knobbly-skinned fruit hanging from their trunks and branches.

As though to welcome Iyer, every green thing swayed and danced in the breeze. A sudden surge of pride rose up in him as he thought of who he was – the scion of gloriously wealthy ancestors! Half-imagined scenes from a bygone era raced through his mind, and he turned eagerly towards Chidambaram.

'Tell me, sir,' said Chidambaram in anticipation.

Shaking his head from side to side, and in a voice brimming with emotion, Iyer declared, 'This is our ancestral property. Our inheritance! And it's not for a mere thirty or forty years that we've owned it, nor just for a hundred or a hundred and fifty years. We have had it for much, much longer! We even have a story about it in our family... and it isn't told just in our house, but even next door and in the house opposite. Actually, they tell this story about us all over town...'

'A little bit of that has reached my ears too, sir.'

'Could be, could be... Seems many-many years ago, there was somebody called Appanna. He had just one son, named Sambamurthi – yes, I'm his namesake! A son born after many-many pilgrimages to holy places and all that. His face used to simply glow like the sun, it is said. Such a handsome boy! But what was the use of it?

'They say that if you are blessed with one thing, you will not be given something else. In his case that is exactly how it was. You know, for eight long years that child did not speak! No 'Appa' or 'Amma' from him; not a single word. Here was a son born through God's grace – but he couldn't talk! What could Appanna do? Indeed, who can understand God's ways?

'Tears streaming from his eyes, Appanna went round the four main streets of the town, giving money away in charity and doing countless good deeds. And did it count for anything? God's grace didn't descend on the boy. Watching the man suffer like that, his noble wife became an utter wreck. She went mad....

'Yet, although he couldn't speak, the boy was very good in every other way. All the work of the temple was done only by him. Another year went by, and the child still didn't speak. The eighth day after that the mother closed her eyes and died. Even before the funeral rites could be completed, the child was missing. Where he went, who took him away, nobody knew. Just a while ago he had been standing there on the street, and all of a sudden he was gone! There was no place they didn't search. They even combed all the rivers and ponds, but there was no sign of the child.

'Appanna broke down and clammed up completely. For two months he wandered the streets like a beggar...'

The accountant let out a yawn.

'How time passes! That dumb boy, a boy who had disappeared god knows where, came back in his sixteenth year, and stood there and spouted divine music. Such nectar!

'His home was now an utter ruin. Nothing was left but broken walls. The lamp that had burned for generations had been snuffed out!

'For a while the child stood looking at the wrecked house. Then, weeping streams of tears, he went to the bank of the Kaveri and sat down under a peepal. That whole day he said nothing at all. Before dawn the next day and for two whole days after that, he sang non-stop. Ah, what music! Like a river swelling to a flood and then flowing softly along!'

Chidambaram settled down comfortably against an iluppai trunk.

'One day passed, then two days, and the third day.

The music kept pouring on and on. It was Narada himself descended on earth. The child's music had summoned up the musician of the gods! But why did the child sing? For whom was he singing? Nobody knew.

'After ten days he left the peepal and the riverbank and went to the Sivan temple. And for many years that was his abode. Ate rice without salt, sang whenever he felt like it, through the night and through the day, he didn't care which it was. But, as the days went on, he sang less, and less, and less.

'One day as he was roaming around with a begging bowl in his hand, a fine palanquin arrived from the king's palace. He didn't raise his eyes to look at it. Three times this happened, before the maharani revealed herself. He didn't get into the palanquin but walked beside it to the palace. But on the eighth day he came running back terrified! 'No, no!' he pleaded with her. 'I am a beggar, a homeless wanderer, a brahmin. All I can do is bless you, that's all, please let me go!' The maharani just melted. Felt very-very guilty, as though she had committed a dreadful sin.

'Now she fell at the feet of the boy and blurted, 'Swami, forgive this ignorant one...'

'And he looked up at the skies and cried, 'Lord! What game of yours is this?'

'Once again the boy began to sing. A song never sung before, never heard before by anybody. Her heart quenched of its desire, the grateful maharani issued a royal grant of this whole forest to his name. This great Saaya Vanam, the forest that can never be felled nor cowed down.'

There were many stories about the original Sambamurthi, and each one was apt to dwell on his piety and his musical genius. It must have changed shape with every retelling. It could be that events were strung together differently each time, some earlier, some later. A living legend of a sage of noble character who not only continuously repeated the name of Rama and who never strayed from the path of righteousness, whatever truth this tale contained took on a new and resplendent gloss from generation to generation.

All that was left of this present-day Sambamurthi's inheritance – apart from his name – were twenty velis of wetland, four groves of tamarind, and some uncultivable forestland. And now that land was up for sale.

'You tell stories really well,' Chidambaram marvelled.

'One can listen all day to Sami when he tells stories,' chimed the accountant.

'Leaves one breathless, the way he tells a story, doesn't it!' went on Chidambaram.

'It's not a story, it's the truth. That's why!'

'Yes-yes!' agreed Chidambaram.

They climbed down from the mound and approached the foot of a punnai. Out flew a babbler with an alarmed shriek, and fluttered over their heads.

'Chhai!' shooed Sambamurthi Iyer, waving it away.

'What do you get out of this forest?' Chidambaram asked him.

'It's just a forest. What can you get from a wilderness? It's just there, that's all,' said the accountant.

'Don't you get anything at all?'

'Ten pails of puli, that's what it gives,' said the accountant.

Iyer was gazing at a gigantic clump of pandanus screwpine, the spathes of their long creamy blossoms open and drooping. The air was replete with a heady fragrance. Two boys were jumping up to reach the flowers.

'What are you doing, boys?' said Iyer to them.

'Taazham flowers, sir.'

'Watch out,' said Iyer. 'Taazham reeds means there'll be snakes. Be careful how you pluck them.'

'Snakes won't come anywhere near us, sir!'

Iyer gave Chidambaram an amused look. The boys were barely thirteen or fourteen. They stood in the middle of the thick clump, waist-deep in the flowers. Although the forest did not belong to them, the use of it was theirs by right.

For whatever grew, and blossomed, and bore fruit in this place, did indeed belong to them. The first spathes of pandanus would go to the temple. After that, two more would go to the Iyer's house, from where they would be invariably be sent to woo a dasi he fancied near Kuttalam. That was how it was with the pickling mangoes as well.

The baby mangoes were never allowed to grow and ripen on the trees. When they were just a month old, they'd be shaken down into a basket suspended from the tip of a slender, hooked pole, and sent to one or the other of the houses he frequented.

The accountant hastened forward past Chidambaram, to ask: 'Are we going any further?'

'No,' said Iyer.

'So… then…' Chidambaram began, and paused.

'What are you going to do with the jungle after buying it?' the accountant demanded. 'Tell Sami that!'

'Oh, that?' said Chidambaram. 'I plan to set up a sugar-cane mill …a small one.'

'Ha ha ha!' they both cackled. 'In this jungle?'

'He is joking, Sami!' the accountant explained to Iyer.

'Looks like that to me, too,' said Iyer, chuckling.

'No, I really mean it. That is my plan, and that is why I'm asking you for this place.'

Iyer spat out his chew of betel upon the kaarai thornbush sprouting at his feet. 'All right. So, you want the forest, don't you?'

'Yes.'

'Take it!' he said grandly.

'Then that's one big part of my work that is all done!' Chidambaram said, with feeling.

There was a silence.

Beating their wings noisily, four or five storks arrived

and settled on branches nearby.

'I never thought it would be settled so fast!'

'Why not?' said Iyer carelessly, holding the edge of his veshti up as he walked on. The accountant cleared a path for him by parting the bushes and creepers. Trampling grass blades and tiny white-blossomed thumbai shrubs underfoot, they crossed several small streams before they came to a road.

As they reached it, Sivanandi Thevar could be seen coming towards them.

'Look, Sami, here comes the Thevar!' exclaimed the accountant. Sivanandi has been in charge of our grove for a long time!' he explained to Chidambaram.

Watching Chidambaram from the corner of his eye, Thevar drew near and remarked to Iyer, 'Had been to the house; Amma said you had come here.'

'Twice I sent a man over to call you.'

'It's about that son of a so-and-so. It's been two years since he deserted that girl. I went to settle that matter once and for all; that's what took all these days...'

'So it got settled one way or other, didn't it? With you going there yourself, how could it be otherwise?'

'I went to a lot of trouble to get it done.'

'That's Sivanandi!' Iyer remarked admiringly to the others. 'No lazy crane waiting for the fish to swim up to him. Gets things done.'

Thevar gave an awkward smile.

'Look here, Sivanandi! This is Chidambaram, he's new to this place. He wants the tamarind grove, and I've promised it to him.'

'The tamarind grove, Sami?'

'You can take care of the garden behind our house from now on.'

'Whatever you say, Sami,' said Thevar in a low voice.

A few pond herons flew past as Sambamurthi Iyer climbed back into the cart and seated himself.

'So, Chidambaram, I'll get going, shall I...?'

'Please come again, sir,' assented Chidambaram, with folded hands. 'Will you be at home tomorrow morning?'

'Yes,' replied Iyer, as the accountant raised the crossbar and fastened it across the back of the cart.

'May I come?'

'Do you have to ask? You are our man now, you can come whenever you want.'

'This respect you give me – I cherish it; I won't let any harm come to it.'

Sivanandi gave Chidambaram a strange look, as though he were seeing him for the first time.

'Coming along, Sivanandi?' asked Iyer. Thevar and the accountant seized hold of the cart and began to walk alongside. No one spoke a word. The cart rumbled past the yellow-blossomed poovarasu and the Ayyanar's shrine tucked away behind the drooping tresses of the fantail palms. When they had left behind the Kaathavaraayan shrine beneath an iluppai tree as well, the accountant observed, 'Looks like Mama is very angry!'

'Yes, yes...,' nodded Iyer, with a sidelong glance at Thevar.

'And why not?' Thevar burst out. 'Couldn't you say one word to me first? Had I crossed the seas and gone abroad or what? I was right there at Vaidheeswaran Koil! Anybody can go there and come back eight times daily, even. If you had sent a man to me, he could have reached me in just two strides, no? So! That's all that this Sivanandi means to Sami...'

'It's not that, da, Sivanandi...' dithered Iyer.

'This man's just good for donkeywork, he's a servant, after all, where is the need to ask him? – is what you must have thought. All right! if this is what you want, do it as you please! But... how did you have the heart to hand over the forest? What are we going to get out of selling it off? Are we going to do what that other landlord, Chinna Pannai, did? He sold off twenty velis of land and squandered it all in Kum'onam!'

Sambamurthi leaned his face on the crossbar and stared wide-eyed at Sivanandi Thevar.

'It is your grove, and you are selling it. Fair enough, but whom are you giving it to? Some nameless fellow who comes from who-knows-where! What is he going to do with it tomorrow? Who knows? I can't help thinking that this fellow is just going to squat on our land and boss us around.

Just wait and see... He and that face of his! As if he's a real scholar and knows all the Vedas! White vaitti and shirt, smart haircut! Stands right beside you as if he is equal to you! And you talk to him, too! Giving him respect!'

Iyer's head wobbled uneasily from side to side.

'This is our earth!' Thevar went on. 'Our forefathers' property! What does it matter if it bears crops or not? Should it go to anyone else, Sami?' exclaimed Thevar. 'If I ask you about it, you can just tell me 'Elei! You go take care of the kitchen garden, da!' Do you have to tell me this? You can tell me, 'Elei! You don't have any garden or land, nothing! Get out da, you donkey!' But even if you grab me by the neck and push me out, I won't go. If you say 'Get out, da!', why should I go? Tell me that, Sami!'

'Four times he came! A thousand times he asked!' pleaded Sambamurthi Iyer. 'I just couldn't say no, Sivanandi.'

'So you gave your word. All right, so that's the custom of your family. To keep your word. But then what's the use of this idiot here, then!'

He glared at the accountant. 'Ei, couldn't you have said, 'Elei! There's no grove here, no nothing, get out!' Shouldn't you have grabbed his neck and given him a good shove?'

The accountant's steps faltered. The cart reached a bend, and gathered speed on the straight road.

'All right, that didn't happen. 'Elei! It's holy ground, there are samis here, you can't wear your smart shirt here.

Bare chest, towel around your waist, that is how you must show respect! And keep a little distance!' Shouldn't you have said that to him at least?'

'I don't know, M-mama...' stammered the man. 'My mind was confused, Mama.'

'Your mind didn't get confused, da ... You and your crowd are the kind who set your own house on fire...'

'Don't say that, please, Mama.'

The cart climbed up the slope.

'Aren't you coming to the house, Sivanandi?'

'There's a job to be done here,' said Sivanandi, giving Iyer a queer look.

'Won't you come tomorrow, then?'

'I shall.'

'I have to discuss many things with you,' said Iyer.

Sivanandi nodded curtly. His mind seething with bitterness, he turned away even as the cartwheels began to move.

Walking beside Iyer's cart, the accountant began, 'Sami, after all, what Mama is saying...'

'Just drop it, will you!' snapped Iyer.

The cart crossed the river, the accountant half-running alongside it.

'Why are you coming along?' Iyer demanded

'Just like that...'

'You may go now. I have some work... Tell Amma I'll be back in the morning.'

'All right, Sami.'

The man's reply failed to enter Iyer's ears and reach the innermost chamber of his mind, where he was already sinking slowly, very slowly, into the loveliness that was Panchavarnam, Shanmugavadivu's daughter.

The cart hastened along the tree-canopied road.

Chapter 02

AS HE TURNED off the road and approached Iyer's house, the accountant's mind swarmed with a medley of thoughts. Trying to sort them out, he was overcome by confusion and doubt. Thevar's reaction to the sale of the forestland puzzled and troubled him. He had had a high opinion of the man's sagacity so far. Now he felt it taking a downslide.

Pushing open the gate, he entered just as Padmavathi was lighting a lamp in the alcove by the side of the doorway. Welcoming him with a nod, she asked, 'Where... Hasn't *he* come?'

'He said he had to go to Neivilakku on some work.'

'Oho!' Her voice trailed away. A smile of contempt and indifference twisting her lips, she gave a knowing toss of her head.

Padmavathi was Sambamurthi's second wife. At seventeen, she had placed a wedding garland around his neck. That had been eight years after his first wife died. He had wedded Padma only after he had got his own daughter married off. In fifteen years, the diminutive young girl who had set foot in his house had metamorphosed into the queen of his household. Now, in the palm of her hand lay all the powers and privileges of that position.

Every night Iyer had to bow his head in supplication before her. He never wearied of it, either. Round and round he went after her, wherever she went. She would give him a look and remark, 'You're simply mad, aren't you!'

'Yes... about you, yes, I am mad!' he would implore.

Pushing away those memories, Padmavathi asked, 'Did he say he'd come in the morning?'

'Yes, amma...'

'That man... he came, didn't he?'

'He was there, waiting. The grove is gone. Sami said he would give it to him, and he has said he will take it. But, look, amma, that Thevar came and threw himself right in the middle!'

'It's our own backyard! Selling and buying it is our will and pleasure! Who is he to get in the middle?'

'That's right, Amma. But it is for Sami to tell him that, and beat him off, isn't it? Sami stays mum, and so he goes on talking and talking!'

'That is *his* business What else, tell me?'

'Only the price has not yet been fixed ...no talk so far about it.'

'Looks like the man has a lot of money, isn't it?'
Yes, amma.'
'Mmm...'
'Singapore-man.'
'I know that!' Padmavathi dismissed the accountant with a smile. So, the amount hadn't been fixed! Possessed by a greedy excitement, she went into the house, trying to decide what price she should urge Iyer to demand of the Singapore-man. Her mind leapt nimbly from one figure to the next, and the next.

Sambamurthi strode in and excitedly announced, 'Look, Padma! It's all done... Five hundred rupees! She got up, startled, and looked uncomprehendingly at him.

'I didn't ask. He himself said it! And I have consented.'

Sambamurthi took out four hundred gold pavuns and the remaining cash, and gave it to her.

'In two days the document must be readied.'

It didn't enter her ears. She was counting the shining new gold sovereigns in a thrill of delight.

'Don't you want any?' she asked him.

'No, not right now.'

Gathering the coins in her lap, she gave him a pretty smile.

'He is a very rich man,' Iyer said. This, too, did not enter her ears.

She picked up two gold sovereigns from her lap and set it before him.

'What for?' he asked.

'For whatever expense...'

Iyer gave her an astonished look. It seemed to him that it was only now, after many days, that she was opening up to him, and it made him very happy.

Yes, he did need the money. In a few days he would need eight sovereigns for some new-fangled bangles. Six months ago he had promised Panchavarnam he would get them for her but it had been put off for one reason or another. Last month she had even held out her bare, bangle-less arms to him and smilingly declared, 'Till your bangles come, this is the way I'm going to be!'

Just the day before, he had received an invitation from her. He had not been able to go until he finished his work with Chidambaram. And today when his cart had stopped at her door, it was her mother who received him, and without the usual enthusiasm.

Iyer seated himself on the swing, and swung himself back and forth awhile.

No sign of Panchavarnam.

At last he asked, 'Vadivu, where is Panchavarnam?'

She smiled coyly, paused for a moment, and then said, 'She can't come out today!'

'Mmm...'

'Only today...'

'Right,' said Iyer, rising abruptly. Flicking his fine gold-bordered angavastram over his shoulder, he went out. But the very next moment, his irritation burnt itself out. There was no sign of his cart at the door. He had sent it away when he entered Vadivu's house. As he stood thinking what to do next, Panchavarnam's cart turned up. He sprang into it, and ordered the cartman to hurry on.

When the cart crossed the Vettaru and came to the bank of the Kaveri, he saw Chidambaram and called out to him.

'Oh, it is you, is it? What brings you here...?'

Iyer's high-pitched laugh crackled out. Betel-stained spittle spurted on Chidambaram's shirt. 'Oh, nothing much! So! Let us finish our business!'

Turning to the cartman, he ordered, 'Elei! Our cart's going along ahead. Just send it here before you go your way!'

When the cart had gone, Chidambaram asked, in a low voice, 'What do you want to tell me, sir?'

'You like the grove, don't you?'

'How is it you are asking me such a thing, sir!'

'Then let's fix a price.'

The other smiled mildly.

'All right... What will you give?'

'It's your property! Shouldn't you be the one to say how much?'

'I don't know all that. I have no experience of it. If you judge it and fix the price, it's all right by me. You have gone around the whole world! Won't you know?'

'Would that be right? You can ask somebody or the other and decide.'

'Why should I ask some other fellow about selling my property? Who is he to give me advice? If I want, I can even give it for free!'

Chidambaram gave him a quizzical look.

'Tell me quickly, Chidambaram.'

'Shall I give you five, sir?'

'Five?' repeated Iyer.

'Yes'

'Right, I agree!'

'Then, please accept this.' From a broad belt at his waist he took out the gold coins and laid them on a stone.

'What is the hurry?' said Iyer deprecatingly. 'After the documents are made out, you can give it to me.'

'Ada, what does it matter where the money is, sir? If it is with you, it is as good as it is with me...'

He counted out the cash. Receiving it in his lap, Iyer said, 'We can get the documents done in two days.'

'What's the hurry for that, now?'

Iyer's cart came to a stop near them.

'Where are you going, Chidambaram?'

'Please go ahead, sir, I have to go on just a bit...'

Iyer climbed into his cart, and said, 'Come over sometime!'

'Right, sir!'

The cart moved on.

Mentally measuring the length and breadth of the land that he had just purchased, Chidambaram walked towards Panchavarnam's house. Her mother welcomed him, overjoyed.

He went in, and sat on the bed. Panchavarnam sat down and leaned against him, murmuring, 'What took you so long?'

'Had some work to do...'

'What is it? Why are you looking at me like that?'

'Just... at you...'

'Me?'

'Mmm...'

From between downcast eyes she directed a piercing glance at him for a moment. Then she passionately clasped his arm, murmuring, 'So you are buying the grove, it seems?'

'Mmm...'

She slid down into his lap and lay there.

03 Chapter

CHIDAMBARAM WAS QUITE sure that Sivanandi Thevar disliked him. And yet it seemed to him that Thevar was the one man who would ensure that he got something to eat in the village.

Food had been a real problem for Chidambaram for the past eight days. After the first day, he simply couldn't down the saltless dollops of gluey rice dished out at the Sivan temple. Nor could he go all the way back to Melapur to Rathna Padayachi's house where he was put up. It was while he was wondering what else he could do that his liaison with Panchavarnam came about. He got tired of that soon, too. He decided that that sort of thing was just not for him, and got out of it.

Increasingly, he began to think about Thevar. Somehow, he felt as if his very life were bound up with Thevar's.

He remembered how Thevar had snubbed him once, and it made him smile. Thevar and Ramasami Chettiar had been standing on the banks of the Kaveri discussing the sowing one morning. Chidambaram stood silently nearby for a long while, but Thevar went on talking as though he had not noticed him. When the conversation was over, he was just about to leave when Chidambaram approached him. 'I've come, sir...' he began, humbly.

Sivanandi Thevar's eyes swept roughly over him. Without giving him a chance to speak, he turned to Chettiar, announcing, 'I'll get going then,' and began to walk away very fast. Chidambaram stood watching him go, longing to reveal to him how they were related. He tried to meet him at his house for two days in a row, but was told 'He has just gone across the river' and 'He has gone to Iyer's house' each time. A conviction that he would somehow manage to see him drove him on now as he strode towards Thevar's house.

On the way, as he neared the iluppai tree, he saw a couple of goats with three gambolling kids, just about a month old. One fell against him. He pushed it away with one hand, and walked on. A dark-skinned boy had leaned his hooked pole against the base of the tree and was chopping down some twigs with a sickle. The feeling that he himself would soon be wielding a sickle grew in his mind as he reached Thevar's house.

Thevar was reclining on a cot across the threshold of his house, the long drooping ends of his luxuriant moustache tucked behind his cheeks.

'Vanakkanga!' Chidambaram brought his two palms together in a respectful greeting.

Thevar looked up, his face registering amazement. Dumbstruck.

'Do you remember me? Chidambaram, sir...!'

'I know! Don't I know!' Thevar remarked, as he shifted a little. 'Sit,' he said, making place for him.

'That's all right,' said Chidambaram politely.

'Just sit down...'

'It's only to meet you that I have come, sir,' said Chidambaram, seating himself carefully on the edge of the cot.

'Seems you had come here earlier too. They told me at the house... I was a little busy... Now, which is your home town?'

He paused to think about it. The town he was born in was Thittakudi, near Neivilakku. If you stood on the bank of the Vettaru, you could see Thittakudi. But he knew nothing of the place. Not a thing came to his mind, although his mother had constantly spoken of it. Five days before she died she had bemoaned, 'Must I die here, out of sight, in this foreign country? This life of mine doesn't even deserve to end in that river where all my people's lives ended!'

And that was the way it was – it was in Colombo that Chidambaram had sprinkled earth on her dead body. Many things had happened to him since then. He had left Colombo and gone to Singapore. When he finally returned to Thittakudi, he couldn't stay there. He landed up at Saaya Vanam.

'Who are your people?' enquired Thevar, when he told him he was from Thittakudi.

'Muniyaandi Thevar...' Chidambaram said hesitantly.

'So! You are Kaveri's boy!' Thevar pushed back his moustache, lips quivering. 'Didn't your mother belong to the Vengapuli crowd?'

'The Mottani clan, Amma used to say.'

'Yes, yes I remember now. That's why I kept wondering for the past four days, who is this thambi? His features are like those of our own people... Adeiyappa! After so many-many years! Come close, sit next to me, little brother!'

'Amma used to keep on talking a lot about you.'

'In a way, I'm a sort of elder brother to her.'

'She told me, 'When you go home, the first thing you must do is meet your Mama, he's everything to us!"

Sivanandi closed his eyes awhile, mulling over it. Like scenes in a shadow play, faded memories wobbled and swayed within him. Indeed, Kaveri was like a younger sister to him. They were from the same clan, the Mottani crowd. He had arranged her marriage himself. A fine family, he had thought then. A good match!

News came one day that her husband had disappeared. Thevar was not at home at the time; he had gone to Seerkazhi town, and couldn't reach Thittakudi until four whole days had passed. Hiding her misery, Kaveri welcomed him and served him a meal. 'Come and stay with us, amma!' he had urged her. She respectfully declined, went out to work, and supported herself and her child. Who knew what went on inside her?

'You were two, or two-and-a-half, when she just left all of a sudden one day for Colombo! Very strong-minded she was, never told anybody anything about it.'

Chidambaram sat on the string cot, scratching at one of the ropes with his finger. He nodded his lowered head in agreement.

'And Kaveri...?'

'Amma's gone cold... Caught the ammai.'

For a long moment Sivanandi Thevar sat with his eyes closed. The ammai – the goddess of smallpox. The mother who burns you, and then leaves you cold.

When he opened them again, his eyelids were moist. In a voice devoid of his usual boldness or cheer, he said, 'Kaveri was a very fine girl. Really smart. Adeiyappa! How hard she could work! She would spin and spin around, just like a top! I have never seen any woman of that age like her.' Memory sprang up afresh, as Thevar plunged into a description of his mother's many excellent qualities.

The more he spoke, the more Chidambaram found himself remembering all the sufferings she had endured not only for her survival, but for his own sake. Hers had been a life of frenetic, unremitting toil, until just eight days before she died. Death was the only calm thing that happened to this spirited woman. It was exactly as though she had just dropped off to sleep... as if she had, as they say, 'gone cold'.

He hadn't even seen it coming. Sitting near her, he had thought she was asleep. It was only later that Annam from next door came in, saw her, and sorrowfully took him outside, saying, 'Amma is gone.' Tears choking her voice, she had hugged him tightly and sobbed.

Somebody quickly came and covered his wailing mouth. They took him away from Annam, somewhere far away. 'Amma has gone cold... She is feeling cool now. So you shouldn't cry, pa,' they shushed, so he never got a chance to cry and give vent to his grief. After that, his eyes stopped welling up altogether. He turned to deadwood within.

'How did you manage over there? Wasn't it difficult?'

'Amma suffered a lot...' Chidambaram said.

'That worthless son of a – ! It ran in his family, that way of thinking! A family tradition it was, to go off and become a holy man! His father went, just like his father's father before him. And then this fellow also went never to come back! Never came anywhere near here. Once we heard that he was in Vadalur for some days, I went there and roamed around for two whole days looking for him. No trace of him.'

'I have no memory of Appa at all, Mama.'

'When he went off to become a samiyar you were a year and a half old.'

'That's what Amma used to say, too, Mama.'

'He used to love you like his own life!'

Chidambaram gave him an odd look.

'Thambi has yet to get married, isn't it?'

With a smile, Chidambaram inclined his head.

Tucking a wad of betel into his mouth, Thevar asked, 'Have the papers been signed for the grove?'

'It was all done just two days ago. Three times I came to see you, but you were not available...' said Chidambaram apologetically.

'What does it matter? As long as everything goes off well, it's all right. They've been talking about it in the village, it reached my ears. But was it proper to ask you about it? And I didn't ask Iyer! I just didn't want to! Twice his accountant came to fetch me. But I didn't go. Why should I go?'

Chidambaram did not venture to reply.

'For forty-five years we have known each other, Iyer and me. His father knew my father, his grandfather knew mine. But those old folks were one kind of people, and he is another sort entirely! Wife keeps him down! So what anyone else says won't even enter his ears!'

A goat kid tripped and fell at Thevar's feet and sprang up again.

'For the past ten days I've been seeing a lot of these

vellaadu goats around here,' observed Chidambaram. The prevalence of this breed of goats had not escaped his eye as he took his measure of the place and its possibilities.

'Has it been ten days since you came here, thambi?' Thevar asked him.

'Twelve days now,' answered Chidambaram.

'And where is Thambi put up?'

'At Melapur Rathna Padaiyachi's house.'

'Where... Padaiyachi's house, is it?'

'Friend of mine in Singapore fixed it up, yes.'

'Who, Govaalan, was it?'

'Yes, Mama.'

'Good-for-nothing fellow! Wasn't man enough to feed the wife he married. Nor the son he brought into the world! Just ran away! Heard he made piles of money over there. That poor woman! Here she's living out her life sweeping in a Paappaan's[1] house. Such times these are! What if she goes astray – and does what that fellow did? But no more of such talk, now...' With great affection, Thevar seized Chidambaram's hand, and declared, 'From now on this is your house. This is where you must stay. Who am I, after all? Whose house is this? Why, I'm your Mama, and this is your own Mama's house!'

Chidambaram's heart leapt up.

---

1   A colloquial pejorative term for Paarpanar (brahmin)

'From now on I won't leave, even if you push me out and shut the door!' he said, happily.

'That's it…that's just the way Kaveri spoke.'

The little vellaadu kid looked up at the tree and bleated a couple of times. Sivanandi Thevar turned towards the house and called out, 'Elei, Chinnayya!' he called his son.

'He isn't here, Mama,' said his daughter-in-law from behind the inner door.

'Kunjamma! Just come here a moment!'

'What, Mama?'

'See who's here …You remember Kaveri, who went away to Colombo? It's her boy – our Chidambaram. And I've been staring and staring at him and asking myself who is this, who is this? Only just now Thambi told me!'

She came out into the front passage, half-hiding behind the pillar. 'I see he resembles that Akka, Mama…'

'Why are you standing over there, Paapa, come over here… it's our Thambi after all!'

With lowered head, Kunjamma came forward. Chidambaram rose, put his palms together and greeted, 'Namaskaranga!'

Thevar and Kunjamma were utterly taken aback: they had never met a man who addressed a woman directly, face to face. How was this to be received, how was it to be responded to? They had no idea. Kunjamma's confusion was greater than Thevar's. She cowered, and retreated a few paces.

Sivanandi Thevar made him sit down. 'Paapa is our daughter-in-law... She is like a mother to you.'

'Really, Mama!'

'You have just arrived. You have still to learn everything... Paapa, you do remember Kaveri, don't you?'

'Why do you need to ask, Mama? Of course I know that akka very well. Twice she has come to our house for a seed-sprouting ceremony.'

'Family ties, people... she liked all that.'

'Tell Thambi this is his home, too. From now on he must stay here with us.'

'When you yourself have said so, will Thambi go against it? Eh, thambi?'

Greatly pleased and contented with the way things had turned out, he said, 'The only thing that troubles me is, why didn't I come earlier!'

'But now here you are... So!'

They all laughed.

'Paapa, we're just going out for a while. Whoever comes, ask them to wait. Come along, thambi,' said Thevar, rising.

'Same features, same walk. That swing of the arms, the look of his eye... the way he stands with his hands on his hips... all just like Kaveri Akka...' They left Kunjamma exclaiming over it.

When they reached the main street of the village, Thevar asked, 'Thambi, you're going to stay here from now on, right?'

'Yes, Mama.'

'Nobody's seen or been to that foreign land – what's so special about it after all? So many fellows here are shouting, 'Me first! Me first!' and running off to that place. Four-five years, and then they come back, grown old and grey before their time, and all worn out... Body doesn't bend as it used to! Can't work like before! So they roam around uselessly from town to town, and when they've spent all the cash in hand, they start picking fights and getting into brawls...and then they end up on the street. Young fellows from here have gone abroad and got thoroughly ruined, thambi!'

Chidambaram listened quietly, with a slow smile.

'It's true, thambi!'

'True, Mama.'

'Were you in Colombo or Jaffna, thambi?'

'Colombo.'

'What was it like over there?'

'Not bad. If you work hard, you can eat well. And you can make some money as well.'

'Isn't it the same here, too? Only, these rogues won't move their lazy bones. They want to catch the best fish but they just skim the surface! How long can that go on?'

'Over there, too, it can't be said that our people work very hard.'

'You light a match and *posuk*, there's your flame! But

work isn't like that. You have to get into the habit of it from a young age. If you've been fooling around aimlessly all along, and then you find you have to go to work, will you be able flex your muscles or bend your waist?'

Shouldering a basket of cowdung, Sornam approached, calling out, 'Who is it, anna?' She stepped aside to let them pass.

'Thambi is related to us. He's the person who has bought the tamarind grove here.'

'This is him, is it? But he looks so young!'

Without offering a reply, they went on, past her. A little way on Thevar said, 'That was Sornam… her story is a strange one. She was one of five children, the only daughter. Pure gold is what she was to them, true to her name; that's how they cared for her, brought her up. Her oldest brother loved her like his very life, and he himself arranged for her marriage. The girl can't be praised enough… she was good as gold, didn't know how to quarrel or scold or speak one loud word, even. That's her character, she got it from her mother. She's fallen so low now, but even now, that quality isn't gone… That's why they say, 'Even in hard times, good people are good people.' But see what's writ on her forehead, thambi! That eldest brother of hers got smallpox and died. His younger brother was like a Pandiya hero of yore, a bold brave fellow, a real treasure – the same Smallpox Goddess, our Maari, she took him away as well. Two broken wings! And just then Ramu, her husband…

your family, thambi! He said he was going off in a boat, and off he went. And only two letters came ...after that there was no news at all. It's going to be ten years now.'

Thevar's eyes brimmed over. That this man could actually weep amazed Chidambaram.

'The year after he sailed away her mother and her other brothers begged her to come home to them. But she's the daughter of a respectable man! Would she return from her married home? No! 'This is my home,' she told them. 'I must die here,' she told them.'

'She's done a lot for that family. When she set foot in that house as a daughter-in-law, her two sisters-in-law were five and six years old. She got them both married. She got her young brother-in-law married too, and that rascal went off to his mother-in-law's house. All alone, she tends to her blind old mother-in-law and lives out her life...'

'Such things happen only to a family that has lived a good life.'

'What you just said is cent per cent right, thambi! But somehow something happens to me when I look at Sornam... Thambi, you lived in Colombo, isn't it?'

'Yes, Mama.'

'There were people from our parts over there, weren't there?'

'Many of them, yes.'

'Did you ever meet Sornam's husband? A dark, hefty fellow, like Bhima himself. Speech was a little slow and stuttering... Name's Ramu.'

Barely opening his lips, Chidambaram gave a gentle smile.

Turning southwards, they went through a thorn gate into a garden, and stood before a small unfinished building.

'Somehow I thought of it, thambi, four months ago. Started to build this house. Didn't know what it was for! And look, today, it seems just right for you. But you've come alone. Soon you must marry, have little ones...'

'In such a short time you have made such big-big plans, Mama!'

'Eye notices something, then the mind starts whirling! But let that be. Thambi, just see if you like the house. Last year in Kum'onam, our Natesa Iyer built a house. This is like that one. When it's finished, it will be really grand!'

About a quarter of the work on the house had been completed. Chidambaram walked around. The house was taking shape just for him... Beyond was a grove of plantains.

Standing on a pile of bricks, Chidambaram asked, 'Is our tamarind grove close to this, Mama?'

'Once you cross the Manakkudi canal, it's all just beyond... the grove, and then the forest... It's all the Saaya Vanam. And what are you planning to grow in your new garden, thambi?'

'Planning to set up a mill, Mama.'

'A mill! In that jungle? What, thambi, are you joking?

What a huge jungle it is! A whole forest! Can any man clear it? Can anyone even think he'll clear it?'

'I'll clear it very fast, Mama.'

'So! If just three-four coins collect in a man's fist, that's what happens! He won't know his head from his feet.'

Chidambaram pretended not to have heard him. Instead he said, 'In a couple of days I am planning to start on this job. I need about ten men. Please arrange for it, Mama.'

'Ten men?'

'If more come, that's good, too.'

'It's the sowing season. Everybody will be in the fields! Men and women both.'

'Five men, Mama?'

'But there's the sowing...'

'What if we pay more?'

Thevar looked up at him, intrigued.

'Just two or three men... it's enough even if they are only boys.'

'I'll take care of it,' said Thevar, at last.

The two of them came out of the plantain grove and reached the threshold of the house.

Chapter 04

EVERY DAY PEOPLE turned up to meet Chidambaram. They asked questions, carried tales, purveyed gossip and banter. From start to finish, every conversation veered around to him. And being subjected to so much attention irked him. Why hadn't he got married yet, they asked again and again, and the question stung him. It felt very much like being roasted and raked over in a hot pan, and it left him speechless. Was it really a friendly interest in him that prompted it all? Or was it just a meddlesome urge to uncover any sleaze there might be in another man's life?

A skinny runt with a gasping voice, and eyes that spun and glinted in their sockets like beads lost in the depths of hell, sidled up to Chidambaram.

'Ei, mapillai!' he hissed, in the ingratiating, jocular tone one might use to a new son-in-law. 'Seems girls are very jor over there?'

Lusty guffaws broke out all around.

Inclining his head slightly, Chidambaram quietly asked, 'Meaning what?'

'Female itself means jor!' yelled a voice from the group.

'Elei, you son of a rogue! What did you say da?' roared Thevar from the doorway. The sheer brute authority in his timbre quelled the chatter. Quickly losing interest, the crowd drifted away much to Chidambaram's relief. He shook out his towel, threw it over his pillow and lay down on his mat.

He had almost nodded off when he was sent for by Thevar, who made him sit next to him on his coir-cot and began, 'Look, thambi, these fellows are plain blabbermouths! Worthless fireworks! They will fizzle out, but they will never light up! 'Give us just some plain mud, and just see how we spin a strong rope out of it,' they'll boast, but when you want any real job done, you won't be able to lay your hands on any of them... That is what they're like, thambi.'

Chidambaram looked intently at him.

'I sent for you to tell you this, thambi. Now go and rest. There's a lot of work to do in the morning.'

He went back and stretched himself out once again. In a short while, the cocks crowed. From the road came the tinkle of bullocks' neck-bells, and the bustle of people up and about. Sleep vanished. With it went the slight chill of the night. Even before he had risen, however, Thevar looked in to announce, 'I'm going to see to the transplanting.'

Chidambaram rolled up his mat and emerged into the courtyard. Kunjamma, who was sweeping it out, stepped out of his way.

Across the Kaveri, past the cremation ground, the guava orchard, and a cluster of huts around a wayfarer's shed, he walked on, with no particular plan in mind. Turning in a south-easterly direction alongside a wilderness of prickly spurges he reached the field where the transplanting was going on.

Thevar wasn't there. They said he hadn't arrived as yet. Wondering where he could have gone, Chidambaram turned homewards. On the bank of the river, astride the path as though blocking the way ahead, stood two dark-skinned, sturdy youths.

'The headman sent us,' they told him.

'What did he say?'

'Said to go and see him.'

'Right, right... You know the puliyanthope, don't you?'

'We know it, sir!'

'Go, have your food, and come there quick!'

'Yes, sir!' The two climbed aboard a bamboo raft. As it moved away, Chidambaram suddenly called out to them, 'Thambi, come here, both of you!' As they came closer, he asked each his name. Then, as though he had just remembered, he asked, 'Aren't you the boys who picked the taazham flowers that day?'

Their faces changed expression. In panic, they both

stepped back.

'There are a lot of flowers there now, did you see them?' asked Chidambaram.

The two of them exchanged wary looks.

'Very big flowers! Go quickly and pick them!'

'Yes, sir.'

'Mmm!'

'We'll come, sir!'

He sent them on their way and returned to the house. Thevar had not come back as yet.

It seemed to him that he could wait no longer. After the noon-meal he took off for Saaya Vanam. Two sickles swung from his right hand. Fresh from Kuppusami's forge, the fine new blades flashed as he walked on. From his left shoulder hung two poles, one long and slender, and one short, with two more sickles tied to their ends. He didn't speak more than a couple of words to those he passed on the way to the grove. Once there, his gaze swivelled around in all four directions.

The boys had not come.

Blocking the view stood a big iluppai tree. He hung the two poles on a branch, and stuck a sickle into the tree trunk. *Chadhak!* The blade leapt into the green trunk, a milky juice spurting from the slash. Wiping away the buttery sap, he retied his vaitti tightly around his loins.

Dry leaves crackled. Somebody was running towards him. He peered intently around, and came face to face with a fox. For a moment it looked at him with its head held up. Then it vanished in a single bound.

'You are all here, too, are you?' he murmured, gazing all around him. Looking up, he could not see the sky at all. The lush green canopy had taken its place. Green above and green below, it was a vista of sky-turned-forest. Slowly, very slowly, he was penetrating this beautiful unspoilt sylvan realm.

A kovai creeper had entirely covered a glossy-leaved poovarasu tree, festooning it from top to bottom and almost hiding it from view. Between the kovai's white flowers were the bright red, oval fruit, bobbing up and down while they were being nibbled at by squirrels. Plunging forward, he saw creepers of many kinds. All the way up a tall nettilingam fir swarmed a kurinja vine. Had somebody plaited this creeper into a swing? The tendrils were so closely woven, it almost looked like the work of human hands...

Catching hold of the 'swing', he gave it a push and stood still for a while. His eyes roved around, trying to penetrate and encompass the wilderness. Abruptly he turned, seized the sickle he had stuck into the iluppai tree, and cut down the dangling liana. One by one he hacked down every creeper his hands could reach. Kovai, kurinja, wild ridge-gourd, the pirandai cactus-vine with its square stalk – he severed them all and flung them away.

But the work he had begun so zestfully soon came to

a stop. Honeythorn and cactus and prickly spurge loomed large before him and barred the way.

He went back to the iluppai. Driving the sickle into its trunk once again, he retied his slackened vaitti. Grasping one of the sickle-tipped poles, he tramped back, slashing at creepers. The sickle couldn't bring down the kurinja vine. All he could do was slash it in two. Both halves remained dangling above.

So a pole with a sickle tied to it was of no use in pulling down these giant lianas! It made him smile at himself. Quickly he sat down and untied the sickle. Out of a poovarasu twig he whittled a short piece of wood and fastened it to the end of the pole with a bit of rope. Hooking this contraption onto a liana, he pulled at it with all his strength. Although the vine loosened a little, it didn't fall to the ground as he had expected. Leaving the pole hanging there and thinking over it, it seemed to him that looking for the roots and destroying them was better than pulling them down.

'That's the thing to do,' he muttered to himself, scanning his surroundings. To the north was a stretch of cacti and nettles – impassable for the present. His gaze swerved westward. There were fewer trees here than in the other parts. Bushes and vines grew layer upon layer, swarming over a big punnai laurel tree and descending from its summit to continue down the other side of the scrub jungle.

Chidambaram took a few steps backward and began his work in earnest. The 'bellyache' castor took the first chop, and fell to earth. Next came the pale purple-blossomed erukku milkweed, and the five-leaved nochi with its cloud-hued flowers. In a single breath he hacked them down, and stepped into a tangle of bristling kaarai. Honeythorn had overgrown the entire forest. Accustomed to surviving in water-starved regions, it thrived and flourished luxuriantly in the moist forest.

Chidambaram advanced, bringing down every plant in his path, one by one. Some plants fell as soon as they felt the sickle, others succumbed after four or five slashes. As for the seasoned kaarai, its stubborn thorns defied the blade.

Each slash resulted in the blade being raised yet higher.

...Tree and shrub and vine have carried on a war against man. Every blow they take from him is a decisive defeat. Yet, they proudly and cruelly weaken their enemy and enervate him, even if only temporarily. Then, when he sits down dejectedly under some tree, some bush, it gently fans him, and showers down a leaf, a blossom...

The sickle slithered from his sweaty palms. He pushed away some leaf litter and gashed the ground with the blade. Picking up a handful of earth and rubbing it on his palms, he took up the pole. Each forceful tug brought down a thick scatter of leaves. The blossoms of the forest dropped down. As he tugged repeatedly at the foliage, a bird's nest tumbled down from the upper branches. He heard a sparrow squeak piteously, in broken snatches. He couldn't see where it had fallen.

Resolutely he went on with his work, until the little bird's ceaseless cheeping finally made him drop the pole and wade into the undergrowth of short date palms. Tramping around searching in all directions, he was stabbed at every step by the long thorns thrusting out from the rough trunks of the palms. Then as he went northwards, he found it: a barely-feathered fledgling impaled on the jagged end of a branch felled by the blade of his hooked pole. He stared unblinking at it lying there for a moment until a screen of tears hid the sight. Then he trudged back with his head bowed, unmindful of the piercing gashes inflicted by the date thorns.

For a while he sat with bowed head under the boughs of a golden laburnum. Hanging athwart a limb facing him was that deadly hooked pole. It swayed in the mild breeze, and did not seem in the least perturbed. With a jerk, he sprang up and seized it. Clasping it to his breast, he looked up at the trees, vines, and flowers.

The lizard-creeper and the ipeca vine had overwhelmed the laburnum. Small white flowers drifted down from the kurinja.

He slung the hook in the middle portion of the vine and begun to tug at it with all his strength, when Kaliyaperumal and Pazhaniyandi arrived. A brief nod of welcome, and they joined him, grasping the pole above and below. They tugged along with him, fraying the vine with each tug, until it suddenly tore away with such force that they all fell on top of each other.

The boys seem to have anticipated this, so quickly did Pazhaniyandi brace himself against falling into the cactus patch. Jumping up, Kaliyan stretched a hand out to his friend and pulled him up. Then he turned to Chidambaram.

'Are you hurt?' Chidambaram asked anxiously. He himself had risen at once after the fall.

'We can even jump down from treetops, sir! Even then we don't get hurt!'

'Really...?' A grimace of astonishment contorted Chidambaram's face.

'There's a 'tirk' to falling... if you fall like that, you won't get hurt, sir.'

A trick to falling! Chidambaram gave an amused nod at the English word that had found its way to a village boy's tongue. Then his gaze fell on the lizard-creeper and the kurinja vine. His thoughts resumed: these creepers could not be pulled down. Muscle couldn't do it, nor could mere cleverness. Creepers are a kind of wizard: they are very strong; they know the skills needed in the sheer struggle for survival. It took real brains to defeat them. If you took the trouble to search out their roots and cut them, there was a chance of winning. For then, in seven or eight days the creeper would wither up. Not that it was easy to discover the root of each vine either.

Kaliyaperumal and Pazhaniyandi were astounded at the sight of the piled-up bushes and creepers that Chidambaram had felled. They exchanged quick winks, and grinned meaningfully at each other.

Pazhaniyandi went up to Chidambaram. 'So many-many plants you have chopped down, sir!' he declared admiringly.

Slapping the boy on the back, Chidambaram said heartily, 'Lots of work ahead for us!'

In tacit acceptance of the work that had fallen to them, the two got busy. They dragged and hauled armfuls of the hacked nochi bushes, the noni-berry trees, the grey-green milky-sapped erukku and the kaarai thorns, all the way up to the foot of the yellow-blossomed poovarasu. It was Pazhaniyandi who had first suggested that spot, and Chidambaram decided on it only after they had all thrashed out their opinions on the matter. From one end to the other, the clearing under the poovarasu could accommodate bundles of lopped-off foliage for hauling away later.

This was only the first step of what promised to be a long and difficult journey, reflected Chidambaram. Or the first scene of a massacre...

No, he decided, he wouldn't let himself think of it like that. Once more, he plunged into the task he had set himself.

This struggle was something he had taken on, out of choice. He and the jungle were now engaged in a fight to the death. He would need all his energy to survive, and triumph over Nature. If he did not succeed, he might as well resign himself to eking out the rest of his life in some obscure hole. It rested in his hands alone: whether or not oblivion was to be his lot.

But they sapped his strength, these bushes and creepers! Fine thorns pierced his feet, burrs hooked themselves on his skin. Brushing against him, the nettles made his skin itch and burn unbearably.

He couldn't give in to these obstacles and cry halt to his journey.. 'I must do something about it... I won't be able to stand it at all tomorrow,' he muttered to himself, as he strained forward to hack at the trunk of a fir. *Juvvvv!* buzzed a swarm of bees, rising up and flying straight at him.

...The blade of his axe had cut through a hive and broken it up. The swarm rammed into his face, forcing him to drop his axe and flee, covering his face with both hands. He ran behind the iluppai and tried to hide himself, but the bees came in phalanxes, one after the other, their concerted hum growing louder and louder. Panic seized him. Breaking out of his hiding place, Chidambaram ran towards Kaliyaperumal.

'A snake, sir?'

'Bees!'

He had hardly got the words out when a section of the swarm came at Kaliyaperumal and Pazhaniyandi. That's the way it is when a hive breaks up: the bees fly around in scattered swarms. The three of them ran back to the poovarasu, stripped off their vaittis and pulled them over their heads. The bees flung themselves against the vaittis and dropped to the ground. Little by little their agitation subsided.

Afterwards, they rested, all three of them, leaning against the poovarasu. They talked about bees, how honey is gathered, and how it feels to be stung. Chidambaram found out many things from the two young boys. It was amazing how much they knew about birds and insects and trees, and how fearless they were.

He shouldn't have panicked about the bees, he thought.

... Yet when he followed them towards the hive, he felt a certain agitation, and hid behind bushes and creepers as he moved along. A large hive the size of a lotus leaf lay on the ground. Another part of it hung from a branch of the nettilingam. Shielding himself, Kaliyan poked at the hive with a long stick and turned it over.

Juvvvv! The bees hovering around it zoomed up and flew around.

'They've seen us! They're coming to attack us!'

'Yes, sir!' agreed Kaliyaperumal. Quickly slipping off his vaitti and cloaking himself in it, he ran straight to the hive and picked it up. A few bees angrily stung him on his hands. He threw the hive to Pazhaniyandi and told him to run with it. Chidambaram could make no sense of what they were trying to do. Bewildered and alarmed, he saw that the swarm was gathering itself together for another attack.

'Run!' yelled Kaliyan.

And run they did, all three of them. They raced all the way to the bank of a pond.

'Is it bad?' asked Chidambaram, taking Kaliyaperumal's hand and holding it in his own palm.

'It stings.'

'Oh, it'll soon be okay,' said Pazhani matter-of-factly, as he squeezed the honeycomb. Honey dripped from between his fingers.

'Ah! Honey!' exclaimed Kaliyaperumal, and stuck his tongue out to catch the drops. 'Very nice!' he said, flicking his tongue out and licking his lips. Pazhaniyandi held the comb out, inviting Chidambaram to catch the squeezed-out drops of honey on his tongue. Chidambaram declined, turned off by the sight of the larvae wriggling in the honey along with the stuff of the comb itself.

When they went back to work, the sun was high in the sky. The lopped-off foliage had begun to wilt. A microcosm teeming with life had come to an unexpected end... But there hadn't been enough sun to shrivel the kaarai. For another day it would retain its fresh green. Hardy by nature, it would last awhile. Yet, in the end it would have to wither and rot and become one with the earth. There was no other way for it.

It was only after he had felled three nettilingams and a punnai that Chidambaram became aware that he was tired. His tongue had gone dry. Taking up the sickle and the axe, he tramped over the trees and bushes that he had himself cut down, and turned back.

Pazhaniyandi was standing next to a short odhiya tree, clasping its pale trunk, while Kaliyaperumal carefully removed a thorn from his foot.

'A thorn?' exclaimed Chidambaram.

'A small one, sir...' Pazhaniyandi answered, wiping away the blood flowing from his heel.

'You have to watch where you are walking! Anywhere you put your foot down there are thorns.'

'You call these thorns, sir! In Rajan's orchard there are cartloads of big-big thorns. Once, two cactus thorns pricked my foot...that's all! But it got all swollen up as if I had elephant-foot sickness! The medicine man told me not to walk for ten days. How could I do that? No… on the third day I began to walk. Swelling, pain, all went away as if it was never there at all!'

'Very strange!' remarked Chidambaram unbelievingly.

'It's true, sir!'

Chidambaram's face softened. 'Go put some medicine on it,' he said, smiling, and they hastened home to have their mid-day meal.

A long distance away, he glimpsed the flowering tips of tall reeds amid the foliage. Those reeds meant there was either a pond or a stream close by... His pace quickening, he finally caught sight of a canal flowing through a thicket of punnai trees.

A gurgling stream running right through his own land! It filled him with elation. But as far as he could make out, there was no way to reach it and get a drink of water. He walked some distance but could see no flight of steps, no slope, and then no canal! It seemed to have mysteriously disappeared.

Then, clambering down a slope trampled by cattle, he reached the water. Scooping it up in both palms he washed his face and quenched his thirst. The water felt refreshingly cold on his face. Wiping it off with the end of his vaitti, he was climbing up the slope, when he heard a voice.

'Are you the one who has bought the land, sir?'

He looked up at the opposite bank, and called back, 'Yes!'

'Two days ago I met Iyer. We started talking about something or other, and then Iyer said, 'Kumarasami, I've sold the forest, da!' I just couldn't believe it! I thought he was just joking, so I said, 'Go on, Sami!''

Chidambaram gave him a sharp look.

'Iyer was saying you're going to set up a factory or something.'

'That's right. A sugar factory.'

'Sugar mill?'

'Right.'

Kumarasami shook his head in disbelief.

'And you're...?' asked Chidambaram.

'Me? I'm from Mangudi.'

'You're the headman of Mangudi, aren't you? Mama has told me so much about you. But why you have stopped on the opposite bank, please come here!'

'That's all right. I was on my way, when I heard a sound. Looked across, and there you were, standing there.'

'Had some work here,' said Chidambaram going down the slope once again, when Kumarasami stopped him with a shout: 'To the south! A log is lying there, come that way!' He indicated the direction.

Chidambaram turned and went southwards, pushing aside the coarse reeds and the grasses. A little distance away, between the iluppai trees, ran the canal and across it lay the trunk of a toddy-palm. A bridge for goats and herdsboys, and even sometimes for grown men, this palmyra 'bridge' was a link between Saaya Vanam and the village of Mangudi.

When he reached the other bank, Kumarasami enquired, in a tone of great courtesy, 'And how are you related to Thevar?'

'I am his younger sister's son.'

'That's what they've been saying... I can see the resemblance, too.'

'Two times I set out to come and meet you, but it got delayed by one thing or another.'

'That's what happens when one starts some work, one by one it'll keep on multiplying.'

'Exactly!'

'Don't I know it! So many jobs we have started, and seen them through too!'

'Mama was telling me only last night there's nothing you don't know about such things.'

'Oh, he's always like that! Goes on saying such things!' Kumarasami grinned, much gratified. 'You don't go believing it all!'

Chidambaram smiled a little smile.

'Is Thevar at home?'

'Yes, he is, please come.'

'I'll do that,' agreed Kumarasami, and quickened his stride. 'We can chat on the way!'

Chidambaram fell in step behind him. An unlooked-for friendship had come his way.

05 Chapter

IN THE OUTFLUNG beams of sunlight, an exquisite day was slowly taking shape.

Chidambaram walked alone into the forest. The trees he had felled the previous day lay prostrate in a dying swoon. Even the honeythorn had begun to wither. Everything was working out well, quite contrary to what he had expected. He felt exultant. Nature itself seemed to be yielding to him, making way most considerately. The ripped vines clung to his feet as he trampled over them to pick up his scattered tools: the hooked poles, the sickles, the axe and the spade. Gathering them together in one spot, he commenced his work.

More than the wild castor plants, more than the nodes of succulent malabar-nut bushes, more than the tight clumps of saw-toothed grass and the flat-leafed cactus with prickles from base to tip, it was the ubiquitous honeythorn that ruled the whole forest. The kaarai grew in such abundance that it had metamorphosed from bush to liana. A marvel of nature, it had inched its way to supremacy by ceaselessly entwining itself around every other plant, tree, and shrub. In the struggle for survival, this plant had crowned itself with a triumphal wreath fashioned out of its own thorns.

Chidambaram steadily mowed it down. Allowing himself to be nicked and pierced by its myriad tiny barbs, he deftly bent back its tough stalks and laid it low. Doing battle with bushes and creepers was getting easier and easier for him. By degrees he was getting to know their every whorl and twist, loop and coil. Seizing a branch of kaarai and bending it with a fluid motion so as to bring down the whole bush with a single chop was a trick he had now mastered.

With as much ease as he lopped the much more pliant malabar-nut shrub, Chidambaram slashed at the kaarai. Little by little, this same kaarai which had been draining him of his strength and enfeebling his knife now proudly surrendered to him, losing nothing of its dignity.

Past the honeythorn flats was a stretch of datepalm, bristling with stiffly outspread, dark green fronds. Each leaflet on each frond was tipped with dark-red spikes. A strikingly different colour scheme, this entrancing new vista spread far into the distance... Mother Earth had bedecked herself anew!

As he bent back a date frond and struck at it, it sprang

back and sent his sickle plunging deep into his left arm. The blood came out in spurts. His face taut with effort to subdue the pain, he put his mouth to his arm and sucked in the blood. The more he sucked, the more it gushed out. Worn out with the effort, he shook his head irritably and untied his vaitti. Tearing off a strip, he wrapped it around the wound. Then he sat leaning against the iluppai trunk.

A fox ran past him, with Pazhaniyandi and Kaliyaperumal in hot pursuit. Shocked at the sight of Chidambaram sprawled out with a big bandage on his arm, they hurried up to him, asking, 'What, sir! You are hurt!'

'Small cut. Sickle touched it.'

'So much blood, sir!'

He nodded wryly.

'My father also got cut like this once, with a big sickle. My mother picked some aadathodai, ground it up very smooth with garlic and put it on the cut. In just two days the wound healed.'

Chidambaram glanced at Kaliyaperumal and nodded. Unwinding the cloth, he retied it and said, 'I'll do that same thing too ...'

'Once I fell from a tree and hurt my knee so badly I could see the bone! That time also she did the same thing. In ten days it became all right.'

'Is that so!'

'Really!'

Giving the boy a hug, Chidambaram said, 'Have you eaten?'

'Yes.'

'Enough cutting for today! Now come, let's pick it all up and put it in a heap!' Chidambaram rose up and led the way.

For the boys, this work was a rousing reprieve from the sheer tedium of having nothing at all to do. Urged on by the ceaseless momentum of the enterprise, they strove to keep pace with the tasks that now devolved upon them, eager to do them justice. With each passing day, the effort gave them a keener pleasure. At the touch of their diminutive hands, the tall gates of the jungle had slowly begun to stir. All that was needed was just to push harder, to persevere and all the mysteries of the primal wilderness would at last lie open to them.

As they felled the timber, the three of them created three enormous heaps, vying with each other in size. As they advanced, they kept glancing back and it seemed to them that they had come a very long distance. They were blazing a new trail. Very likely this was the first time these blades of grass had felt the press of human feet. Stepping carefully on the earth, with its exuberance of loveliness, they went on.

This broad expanse of earth, this very globe, was for man alone! It had been created expressly for his life and for his well-being. In brain and in might man excelled, and through them he brought under his sway this very land once thought to be invincible.

But with every increase in man's progeny, some part or other of the beautiful, blossoming earth inevitably underwent a transformation. Her natural limbs and organs – trees, bushes, creepers, the very blades of grass – were being sheared off and cast away. It was fierce and intense, this warfare between man and the earth. Every day, every moment Nature hurled a challenge. Enticing him with one scent, she led him on to another, she changed tracks continuously, and then she left him stranded, ensnared in an inextricable, tangled mesh. Whenever his strength gave out, it made her laugh.

But there was nothing arrogant about that laugh, it was no triumphant chuckle. It was Nature's last laugh, and it expressed her utter enfeeblement at man's hands.

With pleasant visions of the footwear they would soon acquire, the boys enthusiastically hauled along branches and creepers and piled them up. When they tackled branches too large to haul even for both of them, Chidambaram lent a hand. 'When you grow as big as I am, you can drag them easily as I can!' he assured them.

'You cut down trees very fast, sir! Nobody around here can axe trees like you can!' marvelled Kaliyaperumal. Chidambaram clasped his hand affectionately, and smiled at him.

After the three big heaps of branches had been piled up,

there were still a lot of plants and creepers lying about. Once gathered together, they would make up another couple of heaps.

'What are you going to do with all this?' Pazhani asked, as he tugged along an immense kurinja creeper and deposited it near Chidambaram.

'What shall we do with it? You tell me.'

'We can tell somebody or other to come and take it all away.'

'For what?'

'For manure, what else?'

'Nobody will use this kaarai thorn for manure!' declared Kaliyaperumal.

'What about the nochi? And the noni-berry? The aadathodai?'

'They'll use all that.'

'Then that means half of this will go for fodder. So, that's part of the job done. Both of you go, and fetch someone, quick!' said Chidambaram, as he rose.

Suddenly, from quite close, came the staccato baying of perhaps half a dozen foxes. Hugely delighted, the boys grinned at Chidambaram, whose own face had gone distinctly pale.

'Many-many foxes here! On our way here we saw four foxes, running-running!'

'Mm,' said Chidambaram briefly.

'Sometimes fifty-sixty foxes stand in a group and make

such a racket! Adeiyappa! You can hear it right up to the riverbank. Even we get frightened then. The small boys even clamber up trees, they get so scared!'

'And...?'

'Then we all get together and loudly shout 'Oy!', and the foxes howl back. Sometimes the foxes run away, and sometimes we run away...'

The day fell into a kind of faint. Behind the heaped-up severed limbs of trees, the sky was turning black. Night had arrived: it was not possible to work any longer. Chidambaram said, 'So before it gets very dark, you two go and find somebody to take away the leaves for the cattle. Bring him with you in the morning.'

'Yes...'

As they walked away, the boys loosened the cloths they had tied around their loins and wiped off the grass-blades and leaves that had stuck to their sweating bodies.

'Pazhani!' They turned back at Chidambaram's call.

'Here!' he said, giving them each a three-pice coin. With a hesitant eagerness, they received the money. It was only Thevar Mama and now Chidambaram who had ever given them any money. Whenever Thevar came back from out of town, he would give them each a one-pice coin. They would clutch it for a very brief time before it found its way to Amma's hands. Sometimes she would coax it out of them, and sometimes she would scold and scold until she got it. If that didn't work, she would grab them by their cheeks and pinch until she got the money. What a peculiar satisfaction she got from wrenching coins from her boys!

But not this time. Not this coin! It wouldn't go to her – they wouldn't show it to her! They had obtained it without her knowledge and they were going to spend it as they liked. Each tied his coin into a secure knot at the end of his uppercloth. For a while Chidambaram stood watching them walk quickly away, one behind the other, on the narrow ridge of a distant field.

Then, with no particular aim in view, Chidambaram went towards the cane forest. Huge as it was, it looked even more immense at day's end. It seemed limitless. Leaning comfortably against a lofty punnai tree, he gazed out at the darkening jungle. He could not quite make out what was going on within him, and what was happening without. But every event, every incident seemed to have a message for him....

Pazhaniyandi emerged from behind a bush a little way off and called in a loud voice: 'Kaliyan is fetching the headman, sir!'

'Where?'

'Over there...'

The two of them walked up to a copse of laburnum trees and waited there, under the drooping golden blossoms. Kaliyan's voice could be heard in the distance.

'What are they saying?' asked Chidambaram.

'That the thorns will prick if the leaves are used for

manure. That nobody will go down into the fields, then, for the transplanting!'

'Really?'

'There... they've come!'

A tiger-tooth swaying from the thread hanging at his breast, the headman came near, exclaiming in astonishment, 'Adeiyappa! You have wiped out the whole jungle!'

Chidambaram said nothing to this remark. He stood upright, his eyes on the rising moon. Then he bent and picked up a spotted dove's feather which lay on the ground.

Yes. What he had accomplished so far was not bad at all, he thought. 'But it isn't going fast enough...' Before they could go on with the felling, they would need to finish collecting all that they had cut down and gather it in one place. If someone could be found to strip the leaves from the stalks for easy use as manure, that would be one job done. But the transplanting season was past, and they were already finished with manuring for the year's first crop. If there was somebody who wanted green manure for the second crop, they could carry away the leaves. He didn't know for certain how many would come. The headman could tell him, but from the way he spoke, it looked hopeless. He kept talking at length about how far gone it was in the season. Finally he said, 'Around here, not many people use leaves for manure. But don't you worry, I'll find a way out for you!'

'Won't you take the leaves?' asked Chidambaram.

Sidling up to him, the headman asked, 'They say you are going to set up a factory?'

'A sugar factory... I am planning to set one up.'

'Sugar factory? But sugarcane will never grow here!'

'Really?'

'Yes! Once, Subramania Iyer and Pavadai Padaiyachi planted sugarcane. It just dried up and turned to dust...'

'Really?' said Chidambaram, running a finger through his cropped hair. 'But sugarcane grows in Villiyanoor!'

'Yes, there the sugarcane grows fine.'

'Grows in thick bunches, fine sugarcane!'

'Are you going to bring the sugarcane from there?'

'That's one way of doing it...'

'But there's a river to cross...'

'Yes, so what?'

The headman was nonplussed by Chidambaram's retort. He knew the river, he knew the Kaveri all right. He knew all its currents. From the age of eight, he had driven a cart across it. Even today old Ramasubramania Iyer wanted to be driven across only by him, and would be comfortable only in a cart that he drove.

It was he who rode to Mayavaram from Kaveripattinam on Monday-market days to fetch karuvadu fish for Anjalai, the woman who presided over the local fishmarket. It had been his adroitness and presence of mind that saved a whole precious cartload of four different kinds of dried fish from the swirling floodwaters. And ever since, Anjalai relied on him entirely. She never kept count of the money she gave him. The prestige he enjoyed amongst the fisherfolk was one of its kind, he commanded such respect. Ten days ago, the axle of Singapore-returned Ramu Thevar's rice wagon broke midstream. He had seen it from the riverbank, it all happened in a flash. Many men jumped in and five sacks were saved. But the river swept away ten sacks.

'So, then I'll take your leave,' he said now, to Chidambaram, preparing to depart.

'Some arrangement must be made for this...'

'I'm there to do it.'

'That's good, then...'

'I'll be back.'

'Please come again.'

Pazhani and Kaliyan went along with the headman.

Sitting by himself in the forest, awash in moonlight, he thought it over. His hope that people would turn up to buy the leaves for fodder lay in ruins. If the headman came up with some solution, the work would go smoothly, but right now it didn't look like there was any way it could.

All he needed was manpower. This untamed wilderness was like some great forest of the Vedic times. To demolish it, what he really needed was an army of monkeys, as in the epic, but he must settle for ordinary men, and he was ready to pay good wages. But he couldn't get men! In the afternoon when he had mentioned it to Mangudi Kumarasami, the latter had repeated, 'Men?' and fallen silent.

A raven broke into a frightful cawing. Scrambling to his feet, he uttered a curse as it swooped over his head. He walked ahead, glancing at the piles of felled bushes. Then he looked up at the iluppai trees with their buttery-sweet nut – no less than fifty-two of these trees had to be axed! To spare them was unthinkable. The site for the factory was right there, in the very spot where the iluppai trees grew. That was the place from where to begin, that would be the appropriate point of entry for the whole operation. And to build quarters for the workmen, a brick kiln, not to mention the factory building itself, timber was needed. Iluppai – for every purpose, it was the iluppai timber that would serve best.

Quietly, he made up his mind, and took up his axe. He felt the blade. A thrill coursed through him. A resolve to act, despite the throbbing ache in every part of his body.

First, the stately nettilingam, the mast tree embraced by bushes at its feet and entwined by lianas winding up to its sky-touching tip. With each furious mighty stroke, he drove his axe deeper into its trunk. Like the yellow-blossoming poovarasu, the wood of this tree would never splinter. All its growth was in a single direction: straight up. It grew vertically without swerving to either side. This innocent tree now meekly bent itself to his will.

Whenever the injured arm throbbed, he would sit down and rest awhile, and think about the tree he was going to bring down. Like himself, the tree had many excellences!

If this gigantic nettilingam's entire length fell in a southerly direction, it would land in the cane thicket. Its tip could well reach into the cluster of pandanus reeds. From the direction of its gradual leaning, it looked as though it would indeed fall southwards. This was his first big tree. How many more would he eventually bring down? This was perhaps the only time he would ever be all by himself, in a moon-drenched night, cutting down a tree.

Retreating slightly, he observed the tree and tried to estimate the angle of its descent. His first guess stood confirmed. But across its path stood a solitary toddy palm which threatened to deflect its fall, and turn it southeast to descend among the iluppais. If it crashed down there, it would mean more trouble, more work. He would then have to cut the iluppai and haul it away before he could remove the nettilingam.

Standing to the tree's north, with great deliberation, he swung his axe to administer the final blow. With a loud crack, the tree came crashing down. Racing to a distant point, he surveyed the scene.

The whole jungle suddenly seemed to have been emptied.

The joy he felt was almost too much to bear. Grasping his axe he strode to the fallen giant and walked on it, along its entire length. The night was not yet over, but he had accomplished what he had set out to do.

With the tree brought down and out of the way, the

glitter of the moon and the stars was visible. The sky above exuded beauty's riches, and here below the forest breathed peace. It was nearing dawn, as he strode along, all by himself.

06 Chapter

DARKNESS HAD NOT yet torn itself away, and daylight had not yet completely taken over. Both writhed uneasily in a bleary daze. Somebody, somewhere was calling to cattle, scolding them along. A calf bleated faintly. Birds screeched, and fruit plopped down from branches rustling in the wind.

Chidambaram walked through the darkness into the dense forest. He was in a state of excitement, eager to look once more at the tree he had felled the previous evening. But it was with trepidation that he advanced, step by step, until he reached the gigantic mastwood tree.

Like a woman with loosened tousled hair, it lay prostrate, with outflung branches, more submissive and compliant than he could have imagined. While toppling, it had crushed four or five date palms. Its trunk led straight into the thicket of cane.

At last, it seemed to him that things were falling in

place! Now he could invade and clear that part of the wilderness. Elated, he clambered atop the fallen nettilingam and stood there, fingering the blade of his sickle. Walking along its length, he made his way through the thicket, striking at every limb and branch in his way until he stood in the dark heart of the cane forest. A Trisanku paradise suspended between sky and earth, fringed and canopied by a luxuriance of green cane spread as far as the eye could see.

The sickle proving futile here, he went back to fetch the hooked poles. He soon found he couldn't fasten them on the erect cane stems to pull them down. Each pull caused a rebound and threw him to the ground. Not just the scratch, but the very touch of the cane's minute thorns raised a fiery itch. This was much more irksome than cutting big trees. Yet he doggedly went on with it, bending forward to hack each stem and stretching upward to drag it down.

At last he paused to recline against a branch. Gazing around at the jungle, beyond the expanse of cane, he could see what looked like an open ground, without trees. He couldn't be sure of it. The forest was still sunk in darkness. The sun had not yet risen.

...No, he was certain. This was no dream! That treeless tract was real, he had really caught a glimpse of it! The very thought gave him fresh vigour and energy. He secured his vaitti tightly around his loins and entered the cane thicket once again.

This was uneven ground, with no place even to stand and pull down the cut cane stems. Twice he tugged, and twice the cane sprang back and hurled him down in mortifying fashion. Rage mounting within, he rose abruptly and began to collect branches of the fallen nettilingam. Carefully he arranged them to protect himself against falling. Now he had a place to stand, and to brace himself against the cane's assault.

A slight smile formed on his lips.

Methodically, he persevered in a northerly direction. The cane in that stretch had grown profusely, in a circular formation, around two long-fallen palmyras. Beneath the trunks extended a kind of tunnel. A rare occurrence indeed in a cane forest! Surely, luck was on his side – and if he sat down in the tunnel and pushed himself, half-sliding and half-crawling through, maybe he would reach the other side of the forest. There was no certainty about it. He took the smaller hooked pole and his hack-knife and set off. The first stretch was all right, but as he went further, more and more cane-stems blocked his way until there was total darkness. The cane had sent out lush shoots of vines enmeshing the whole palmyra tree in its coils. There was no way to go on with the journey.

Sitting there, inside the 'tunnel', Chidambaram pondered it over for a long while. How far had he come? He had no way of knowing, but it struck him that it could not have been not very far either.

Again he slashed at the cane, this time hacking away at the base, using both the hooked pole and the hack-knife. Again he was thwarted by the cane's sheer exuberance. It rendered him powerless even to raise his knife-wielding arm. The cane was destroying his ardour. It taunted him, mocked all his effort.

With a deep sigh he turned back. What he had planned was just not happening. His desire unconsummated, he turned and went back to sit under the iluppai tree.

A ray of light appeared on the edge of the sky and spread in a vague shimmer through the forest. The screeching and fluttering of birds grew louder. Slinging his hooked pole on a branch, Chidambaram stripped away the cloth covering his wound. The two ends had come together. It would heal in a few days. He undid the bandage and neatly retied it.

'Namaskaranga! Seems you asked me to come?' called out a voice. Chidambaram looked up. He had never seen the man, but he had been expecting him to turn up. Yesterday when he called on him, he was out, and Pazhani had regretfully said, 'Just now only he left for Chettiar's house, sir!'

It was Pazhaniyandi's father Arumugam who stood before him now. He had his son's eyes, face and features.

'Pazhani has been working here for some days,' he began.

'Yes, he has ...'

'Who is the boy working with him?'

'Sister's son. Stays with us.'

'Very good friends!'

'Everybody in town says so.'

'It is really true,' he said.

Going up to him, Chidambaram said, 'Why I called you was, the boys are doing good work, I'll give them a little something, let them stay here. This is what I wanted to tell you...'

'That is all right, but our family has been working for the Chettiar for generations. The Chettiar from the big stone house.'

Chidambaram fixed him with a level gaze. 'All right. But when they have let the cattle out to graze and have nothing to do, let them come here and do a little work.'

'How can that be?'

'Why not? I'll pay wages.'

Arumugam grinned, showing misshapen, betel-stained teeth. 'They are only boys, after all! What big work can they do, for you to pay them wages!'

'What sort of talk is that! Work means wages! And I will also give them three measures of paddy!'

'Let it be as you wish. The headman had told me about this, and now you are saying the same thing too. What can I say?' Arumugam appeared pleased enough. But his face turned serious, as he added, 'Whatever happens, please put in a word first with Chettiar.'

'Who... Kanakasabai Chettiar?'

'Yes.'

'I will tell him. If you want, I will also ask Mama to talk to him.'

'Oh, no need for that! If you say one word, it will be quite enough. He won't say anything. But I shouldn't do anything without him knowing, isn't it? That's why...'

'That's there, yes.'

'So, I'll take your leave.'

'Come again.'

Arumugam had taken just a couple of steps when Chidambaram called him back. 'We need some men to cut down the trees. If you find anybody, please send them to me.'

'In our village, only Pandurengu used to cut down trees. Adeiyappa! He could hew down any tree in just four days, whatever the size. But look at the pity of it: One of the trees he cut down turned out to be his own Yama! It was his unlucky time. After that, the number of woodcutters in this place has shrunk to nothing. Nobody here chops down trees any more. Nowadays it's only the Villiyanoor men who come here and cut our trees.'

'From Villiyanoor?'

'Yes, Appusami and his younger brother. Those two are big strong fellows... But I've heard that they have gone to some other country. I'm going that way this evening, I'll find out.'

'Please be sure to tell them.'

'I'll tell them, so shall I leave now?' said Arumugam, and departed.

Chidambaram shrugged away the flowers that had drifted down upon his head and looked up. In the morning light the golden kalasam atop the Mayavaram temple glittered in the distance. That magnificent pot-shaped finial was of unusual size, as was the temple itself. Built by the Cholas who had made Thanjavur their capital, the Mayavaram temple had gained considerably in prestige and power at the time of the Nayakars. A kind of glory had come to reside in the town, like a gem embedded in gold. The villages of Saaya Vanam, Neivilakku, Mangudi, Villiyanoor, Malliyakollai and Melakaram looked upon Mayavaram as their mother. Together with Kumbakonam and Seerkazhi, Mayavaram formed a triangle within which a whole way of life was contained.

Mayavaram's bazaars, Kumbakonam's great Festival of the Tank – his mother had always talked about them. Every year in the month of Aippasi, her thoughts would drift to the banks of the Kaveri. Those were the days when vague dreams and ideas were entangled in his mind. Although he didn't really understand the emotion with which she spoke, he would sit by her and listen to everything she said. That he was listening was enough for her – it made her happy. None of her stories really impressed themselves in his mind. Each chased away the next, till none remained...

Years had passed, and Aippasi was coming around

once again. Back among his own people, their ways and customs were rubbing off on him – all except for those which had to do with religion and 'god'. Confusion was the predominant feeling in his mind when it came to such things.

For he felt he had turned into a kind of mongrel. There were two religions grappling within him, and both had seriously damaged him. By virtue of his birth he had inherited the Hindu Sanatana Dharma, the 'eternal religion', but what had been dumped on him was its grandeur and its orthodoxy, its compassion and its cruelties, and its untouchability – its good and its evil. To shake it all off and go on his way was impossible. He had tried it. But his legs buckled and grew numb, and he had returned to the fold, all alone.

His life was a strange story, full of amazing twists. Whenever he remembered his childhood, Chidambaram would suffer in silence. A harrowing memory of what he and his mother had endured on the tea estates would rear up and threaten to engulf him. If only she had lived! He would have surely seen to it that she enjoyed every comfort, every luxury he could ever buy! And then his musings would take an abrupt turn – if indeed his mother had survived, would he have had this life he was now living?

She had died of smallpox. The disease splattered over her in a scalding downpour, and then she cooled off forever. He had sat staring blankly at the corpse until a dark-skinned preacher took him away with him. He did not resist, but it did take him even four days to reconcile himself to his new situation. The preacher harangued him about the meaning of life and about the Creator, and took him to church. They sheared off the long hair through which his mother used to run her fingers. A white preacher appeared and bestowed a white upper garment and a khaki lower garment on him. He didn't know how to put it on. He put both his feet through one leg of the shorts and struggled with it until the preacher came to his aid. He was baptised, ceremoniously ushered to a seat – a real chair! – in the church,[2] the 'abode of wisdom'. He received a new name – David Chidambaram. Without the least twinge of regret, he removed the ruby kadukkans from his ears and gave them up. He liked the church school very much. Once he started going to school, he hardly ever thought about his mother.

Eight years later, the black preacher took him out of

---

2 Kandasamy employs the popular corruption of the term for baptism, gnaanasthaanam. Converts have often been drawn from the poorest and most oppressed castes, as also women. The idea of a Christian congregation of equals seated together seized the imagination in a society where the hierarchical caste and gender structure made it unthinkable for them to sit down with their social superiors. Thus gnaanasnaanam or the bath of wisdom, the sprinkling of holy water, has become gnaanasthaanam, alluding to the elevation in status on conversion, when a person becomes worthy to sit in church, in a place of wisdom.

school and put him to work in somebody's house. Three months of that was all that he could stand: he stole ten rupees and left for Colombo. There, for close to a year, he flitted from job to job.

He also fell in love. It happened in church. Three years older than him, she was married and the mother of a child. This woman, who kept saying that he was her very life, drove him out nine months later. Maddened by her jeering contempt, he followed her four Sundays in a row. She would turn and glare at him, and walk rapidly on.

His path veered away from church. Looking for employment, he finally found it in Siva-shanmugam's pots-and-pans shop.

'What's your name?' asked Siva-shanmugam.

'David Chidambaram,' he answered.

'What's this 'David'! Just Chidambaram is enough!' Siva-shanmugam had retorted. And he had nodded silently.

'There's some vibhuti over there, smear it on your forehead!' said his new boss, pointing to holy ash in the shop's altar. Afterwards Chidambaram accompanied him to the temple at Kadirgamam. But by the time he left Ceylon, holding on to belief in any god at all had become a problem. He had no yen for any religious experience. None of it seemed to have anything to do with him.

He had no nostalgia for any of these experiences with religion. He behaved as though none of it had anything to do with him.

It was now a year since he had returned to his birthplace. Some powerful force kept him from entering any temple. He often thought about it but couldn't quite figure out what it was. Bhadrakali, fearsome and beloved, under the iluppai tree in the Paraiyas' quarter, the hunter-god Periya Karuppu of the Thevars, the uppercaste Hindus' Saneesvaran who must be propitiated to ward off ill-luck, the Sivan and the Vishnu of the brahmins... People went to one or the other of these temples whenever they felt the need, making no distinction at all between these gods. What was this force that stopped him from going to any of them? It disturbed him to think of any God having limitless power.

A couple of days ago, before they went to the Mariamman temple to offer oil-lamps fashioned from rice dough, Thevar's daughter-in-law Kunjamma had asked Chidambaram to come along. Having talked to him repeatedly about it, Thevar went on ahead, telling him to follow. For a brief moment, Chidambaram had even considered going along.

Until he thought of something else he had to do.

'I'll just go quickly to Pattamangalam Street and be back, akka,' he said to her, and rushed down the steps. By the time Kunjamma stepped out of the front door, he had turned the street corner.

He was the only one in Saaya Vanam without a kudumi. He had cut off his tuft and wore his hair cropped short. For days on end people gave him strange looks as he went around with his forehead bare of the usual streaks of holy ash, and wearing a shirt, unlike other men who went around bare-chested. They had kept him at a little distance.

Now, however, he had charmed them all.

A flower dropped on his head from the poovarasu tree. Tossing it off, he tested the blades of the hooked pole and the sickle. They had gone blunt, but the axe was not too bad; the edge would stay sharp for another four days of work. What was needed right now was to get the sickle and the scythe sharpened, or even hammered in a forge. With the idea of taking them to a blacksmith, he set off for the riverbank.

Subburathnam Iyer and Patanjali Shastri were standing by the Kaveri. For the past ten or twelve days Subburathnam had had a yen to meet this Chidambaram, about whom everybody told such stories. He had looked for him all over, but hadn't had a glimpse of him. Patanjali Shastri had seen him a couple of times, but had had no chance to speak with him.

Melakaram Parthasarathi Iyengar, on the other hand, had struck up a friendship with Chidambaram within eight days of his arrival in the village. He had taken quite a fancy to him, and chattered on and on about him every opportunity.

'Oy! Have you met that Chedambaram yet?' he would exclaim, laughing and slapping Patanjali Shastri's thigh, as they lounged together playing cards on some thinnai in the brahmin quarter. His voice could be heard four houses away.

'Who is this great man – some white lord? Why must I go and see him?'

'You go and talk just two words to him and then tell me what you think!'

'Why, is he so special? Grown two horns on his head?'

'Oy! A fat lot you think of yourself!' Iyengar would retort, flinging down the cards in his hand – just as he always did when he didn't have a good hand. The game would break up, with the gentlemen rising abruptly, clutching their slackened veshtis.

Now, at the riverbank, as Chidambaram approached, Subburathnam enquired, 'You're Chidambaram?'

Chidambaram greeted him with folded hands. 'You are the Iyer of the banana grove, I think? Mama has told me so much about you. I called on you twice, but couldn't meet you.'

'Doesn't matter... We know Sivanandi very well, he's our man. When he said, 'My younger sister's son has come here,' I asked, 'Where is he?' and he kept answering 'here he is' and 'there he goes!' but I never set eyes on you till just now! D'you know this gentleman? Patanjali Shastri?'

'A little...but only by sight.'

'So, you've roamed all over the country and landed up here, is it!

'Not really...'

'Bought up that grove without a third person knowing anything about it!'

'Somehow, it all happened so quickly.'

'What are you going to do with the grove?' demanded Patanjali Shastri rather gruffly.

News of Chidambaram's plan of starting a sugar factory had spread throughout the village, but few believed it. A rumour was afloat that it was just a cover for some murky business. One report had it that he was going to dig a tunnel and mine for gold, and another that he was going to clear the forest and give the land to the railway people. Nobody knew who concocted these stories. Thevar would chuckle over them, but Chidambaram couldn't bring himself even to smile – they annoyed him so much.

Today, however, he wanted very much to laugh. Controlling himself, he said, 'I'm going to build a sugar mill.'

'That is what they are saying in the village,' said Patanjali Shastri, turning to Subburathnam with a meaningful wink.

'Will sugarcane grow here, Chidambaram?'

'I think it will, sir.'

Subburathnam's guffaws bubbled up like water on the boil. You see our Shastri here? Eight years before you he planted sugarcane – two whole velis of it. You could span it with one hand, it grew only that high, and then it just dried up.'

'I'm the first fellow to plant sugarcane here. And the last, till now. Don't know why, but that's how lucky this soil is for growing sugarcane!'

Chidambaram listened in silence to all that they had to say.

'Plant banana. It'll grow fine.'

'D'you know how many types grow in this soil? There's rasthali, and mondhan...'

'Really, sir?'

'They even call me Banana-Grove Iyer!'

He gave a slow smile.

'Why can't you plant banana?'

'Not that I can't... just that I haven't given it a thought so far.'

'Think about it, properly, not just once, but twice! We hear you're a much-travelled man, been to four-five countries. Like a little sparrow you have searched here and there and poked around and picked up and earned a few coins. If something goes wrong here tomorrow, what will you say about us? So many people were there, why couldn't they have said a word about it? That's what you'll feel like saying then. Can't say it's wrong, either. People's minds think in four-five different ways, tongues talk four-five different things.'

'Many thanks... I am not about to do anything in a hurry, sir. Everything will happen slowly. First, I have to clear away the trees and the timber. That's the first job.

Only after that comes the rest of the work.'

'Clear that forest? It is thirty generations old! No man who goes into it comes back! What did you buy it for? Couldn't you have asked me a word about it? I myself would have given you twenty velis by the side of the road!'

'Had no idea.'

They stepped forward. It was clear to Chidambaram now that his business with them was over, so he took his leave of them and walked quickly away. Two trains of thought went through his mind. First thing he had to do was to meet Kanakasabapati Chettiar. Then he had to collect some sickles, spades, hooked poles and axes.

It was time to start work. The 'dark season' was past, the rains had cleared. But until a new set of workers arrived, the work would not proceed apace. Rather than depend on others, he would have to toil all by himself.

Not that the prospect dismayed him in the least.

Chapter 07

A NANNY GOAT and her two kids clung on to Sivanandi Thevar's legs as he picked tender leaves from the odhiya tree in his front yard.

'Cutting leaves, Mama?' Chidambaram's voice was full of affectionate respect. Thevar tugged at a small branch caught in his hooked pole and said, 'Oh, is it you, thambi? Rascal of a goatherd has gone off somewhere, leaving this poor thing here. She's just given birth to these two. Just listen to her bleating.'

'Give it here, Mama,' said Chidambaram reaching for the pole.

'No need, thambi, just a couple of more twigs to break.'

'Why, can't I pluck them?' demanded Chidambaram. Prising the pole from Thevar's hand, he quickly twisted off several sprigs and pulled them down.

'Enough, thambi, enough! She's just given birth – if she eats too much she'll purge.'

'Oh?' Chidambaram laid aside the pole and sat down with Thevar on the cot. He leaned close to him and said, 'At least one job's done, Mama!'

'Saw the Chettiar?'

'Yes, I went to him and said please, you must leave Pazhani and Kaliyaperumal with us here for some days. 'What relation are you to Thevar,' he asked me, 'how are you connected?' Sister's son – that's what you could call it, I told him. And that was it – he became so happy! Face just opened up like a... like a flower! The boys are yours now, he said, they'll follow you like two tails!'

Fully conscious of the compliment to himself, Thevar acknowledged it with a genial smile, whiskers twitching with pleasure.

'Our Chettiar is a fine man, thambi. You know, no one can match him here, in our whole neighbourhood. As good as gold, you might say. He even had a golden kalasam made for the Avaiyambal temple tower! And he renovated the Mangudi Pillaiyar temple too. For the Thai Poosam festival at Vadalur, every year he always sends two cartloads of rice and one of provisions, before he himself reaches there. They'll be ready and waiting!'

'So, he has a lot of wealth, isn't that what you're saying, Mama!'

'Wealth? It is just one hundred velis of wetland and sixty of dryland. Ancestral property. And another hundred and fifty velis that Aachi brought in as dowry. The funny part of it is that if you ask either of them where all this is, neither of them would know! All this reckoning is just guesswork.'

Chidambaram had seen the two schools that Chettiar had established. He rather liked the school for Vedic studies. Actually, he had found, on asking around, that Chettiar hadn't actually set it up himself. Already an old institution, it had been functioning for two generations but had closed down eight years ago for lack of teachers. The pandit of the school, Balasubramania Iyer, refused to give up on it, though. He had trudged around the entire Brahmin quarter pleading for help. None was forthcoming. After waiting for a couple of months, he finally went to Chettiar's house one morning, and made a dignified appeal.

Chettiar donated his own eldest uncle's house and the income from one and a half velis. Then Narayana Rao came forward with a quarter kaani of land. Murugaboopathi Pillai ten kuzhis, Kalyani Aachi three maas, and Kuppaiyur Ramanujadasar two kuzhis – funds now began to come in.

Chidambaram had seen the pandit once. Around eighty years old, with beard, moustache and eyebrows all gone white, his wan frame was thin as a stick, desiccated by rigorous austerities and his brahmacharya's vow of celibacy. It was not his body but the stentorian timbre of Balasubramania Iyer's voice that compelled attention. It rang out like a bronze bell. When Chidambaram looked in at the school, he had found him conducting a Sanskrit class. He couldn't understand any of it, but he had liked the voice, and he liked the man.

Yet, Chidambaram did not get carried away. 'This kind of life leads only to utter emptiness. It's terribly backward-looking,' he told himself. How different his own life was, with utterly novel experiences of which his father and his grandfather could never even have dreamed! Two religions had moulded his way of thinking. This was a whole new way of life. He was the first on that road – a pioneer! Sitting there with Sivanandi Thevar, he felt the thought expanding and occupying his entire mind...

'Thambi?'

Ramasami Thevar's voice disturbed his reverie.

Sivanandi Thevar demanded, 'Yes? Now what brings you here?'

'I'm off to the jasmine garden, Mama.'

Pushing his pendulous whiskers back over his cheeks, Sivanandi Thevar said, 'Tell that boy with the handsaw to come at once. Four times I've sent a man to fetch him, but he keeps giving me the slip.'

'I'll tell him, Mama, but I think he's gone to Kuttalam town.'

'Boy's gone away to Kuttalam, has he?'

'Yes, Mama.'

'All right, just let him come back here. Where else can he go, after all? I'll take care of him then!' said Sivanandi Thevar. 'Elei, Ramu! I told you to arrange for two sacks of first-crop paddy, didn't I!'

'All right, Mama.'

'Don't forget!'

'When Mama says something, how can I forget it?'

Chidambaram raised his head and looked at Ramasami.

'Thambi here doesn't say a word!'

'What do you want him to talk about?'

'You asked right!'

'Here I am, asking you something, and you laugh as though I'm asking somebody else!'

'Whenever Mama talks, I feel like laughing!'

'Oh, is that so?'

'I'll take your leave, thambi!'

'Please come again,' said Chidambaram rising from the cot and folding his hands courteously.

After he was gone, Thevar laughed sardonically. 'What are you giving him all this respect for?'

Chidambaram's eyes narrowed.

'Why give him respect simply because he is related to us?'

To which Chidambaram said nothing at all.

Kunjamma called from within. 'Here, I'm coming, Paapa!' answered Thevar, rising and handing Chidambaram a pitcher to fetch himself water. Chidambaram washed his hands and feet and followed him inside. In the alcove was holy ash; he helped himself to a handful and smeared his brow with it.

'Your stripes are bigger even than mine!' declared Sivanandi Thevar.

'I don't know how to do it properly, Mama, I have forgotten the habit!'

Laid out on a strip of plantain leaf was soaked cold-rice and a bowl of thick buffalo-milk curds. On one side of the leaf was well-simmered tamarind gravy, and on another was a piece of driedfish, roasted black, and giving off a strong aroma. With one finger, Chidambaram pushed it away and began to eat.

Thevar was eating away by his side, oblivious. 'What, Paapa? Isn't there any shrimp powder?' he asked. Paapa, 'little one', was what he called his daughter-in-law, and his granddaughter as well. Teasing them by calling them by the same name was becoming more and more of a habit with him.

'Here, Mama!' she called, quickly emerging with the shrimp relish.

'Give Thambi plenty of it. So many big cities he has seen, maybe he will like it or maybe he won't... Adadaa! What, thambi, you haven't eaten the seerfish, you've set it aside!'

'It's vanjira!' protested Kunjamma.

'Look, thambi, of all fish, seer is the very best. Just eat it roasted it to a crisp, and you'll think poorly of even the nectar of the gods!'

'This fish doesn't have a single tiny bone, thambi!'

coaxed Kunjamma.

Peeling off the burnt black skin, he broke off a small moist piece and put it in his mouth. 'It's very good!' he agreed.

'This kind of fish actually has a fine smell of ghee' Thevar declared, and instructed Kunjamma to serve Chidambaram two more pieces. He did not insist on refusing it.

It took a long time for them to rise from the meal. A faint reek of fish clung to his hands, even after he had washed his hands after smearing them with plenty of coconut oil. Reaching for the tray of betel leaves, Thevar asked, 'So, thambi, what have you been doing in the grove for the last couple of days? We never see you here at all...'

'One or two bushes, one or two branches... I cut a bit of this and a bit of that... Work is going on little by little, Mama.'

'That's the way it is. We have to keep doing at least something.'

'The sickle has gone blunt, though,' he said modestly.

Thevar gave him a look of warm admiration. 'We have four sickles in the house. Six can be got from Ramu Thevar's house, hmm... and then there are five or six sickles in Samikannu Padayachi's house, we can get those as well,' he offered. 'More than enough, Mama!' he exclaimed, gratefully. 'But we also need a few spades, axes, and hooked poles.'

Sivanandi Thevar quickly took in all that he had to say, his mind responding to Chidambaram's tone of urgency like a wheel set in motion. 'We only have to put in a word to ironsmith Thangasami. In just four days he'll make them and deliver them to us. We can look in on him on our way out.'

'Are you also coming to the grove, Mama?' asked Chidambaram, eagerly.

'I must go and see just what Thambi is doing in the grove, mustn't I?'

'Certainly, Mama!'

When Thevar returned from Ramu's house with the sickles, Rajathi from the house down the street said, 'Mama, I want two plantain leaves.'

'It's in my lap, come close, I'll untie them and give them to you!'

'Go on, Mama! Teasing me!'

'What for are you making a face, di? If you want leaves, go cut them for yourself! Instead you are asking an old man to do it for you.'

She gave a bashful smile.

'Oh! That's what it is! Who has come?'

'Alamelu's husband, from Movoor...'

'And who is this husband of Alamelu's? You mean your younger brother-in-law...'

'Go on, Mama!' With a quick sinuous movement, she turned and glided away, only to return, calling, 'Mama!'

'What is it, Rajathi?'

'Will you be going towards the marketplace?'

'What for?'

'Guests keep coming, we need provisions.'

'It will take me two more days to go that way. But Paapa had been to the shop only yesterday.'

'Then I'll just go and see akka, Mama!' She walked rapidly away.

There were two provision stores at the southern end of the Saaya Vanam village. One was Appu Chettiar's, the other Mogadeen Rao's. Beyond these two, at the tip of the village of Neivilakku was Komutti Chetti's shop. Komutti's was known more for medicines rather than for provisions. Its specialty was a herbal concoction for women who had just delivered.

Basic provisions could be procured within the village. What was not available – particularly millets like bajra, ragi and thinai, as well as sweet potato – was brought in on bullock-cart by outsiders and sold in Saaya Vanam. The villagers simply bartered what they had in excess for the goods they required. They never had to go to a store to buy tamarind. Thevar only had to shake it down from the trees in Iyer's grove and have it sent to them. Chillies grew in their own backyards. The Chettiar traded gingelly oil for horse-gram, and there was no real measure. You went to the oil-press and took as much as you wanted; nobody would ask you the why or wherefore of it. It was as though it were your own oil-press, just as much as it was your own horse-gram. It was only for buying clothes that you had to go to Mayavaram. And that was ten miles by foot. If you went by bullock-cart you could alight at Chettiar's doorstep. The loom in Chettiar's house was as good as your own — any time you wanted you could pick up a vaitti or a sari or a towel, and repay him in grain, along with others in the village, well after the harvest.

Nobody kept an exact account; it was just memory of the spoken word that did the calculations. For these people believed in word of mouth. Their whole lives were built on what they said, or was said to them.

But something happened to test this premise, an event that cast them into utter confusion. Venugopala Iyer's son Krishnan went to study in the city and then took off from there to go to England, that far-off 'Seemai' beyond the seas. It plunged the entire brahmin quarter into a state of shock and humiliation. Every brahmin household behaved as though a death had taken place within its walls. If Krishnan ever came back, they said loudly, he would be excommunicated from their caste! They ostracised his father for almost a year. It was only after he disowned his son that the taboos were relaxed.

At dawn one day, Krishnan returned with big suitcases and plenty of money. The outcries against him subsided. A strange thing happened. Those who had condemned him now declared that the shastras recommended rites of expiation for such transgressions as crossing the black waters. For three days sacrificial fires blazed in their house. From Mayavaram, Melakaram, Neivilakku, Mangudi, and even further, a hundred brahmins, adept in the Vedas, came over to conduct the proceedings. Only the venerable Balasubramania Iyer stayed away. although he was from Saaya Vanam itself. Two months after he had been cleansed of his sins, Krishnan went to the big city and married a Christian girl in a church. This news greatly disturbed Saaya Vanam's residents.

And before that tidal wave had quite receded, Chidambaram turned up. Here was a man who had crossed the sea, travelled in many lands. For him, however, there were no caste taboos or restrictions. His was a different caste, and its values were different. He was not a person who could turn Saaya Vanam upside down, as Krishnan had. He had come with a plan of action for the village. And he enjoyed considerable support.

Taking down the sickle from its hook in the passage, he went to the iluppai tree to pick up the hooked pole. It was very long and somewhat heavy, and because he was not quite accustomed to balancing it, it dangled in an ungainly fashion from his shoulder.

'Give it to me, thambi...'

Chidambaram hesitated.

'That pole! Just give it here...' Sivanandi took it from him, slung it effortlessly on his shoulder and walked ahead.

'How that thing wobbled and shook when I was carrying it! But it isn't moving even a little bit now!' remarked Chidambaram.

'It's nothing... just practice. In ten days you'll also carry it like this.'

'Me?'

Turning abruptly towards him, Thevar emphatically declared, 'There is nothing that Thambi cannot do! Do you know that?' Momentarily taken aback, Chidambaram gazed wordlessly at the older man.

They walked on. Somebody came up behind them.

'What's all this, anna? Carrying a hooked pole and going somewhere?'

'I'm just going to his grove, Sornam! You know who this is, don't you? You know Iyer's grove – this is the thambi who has bought it.'

'So, this is that thambi! Namaskaranga, thambi!'

'Namaskaranga.'

'Sornavelu Padaiyachi...' Thevar introduced him. 'Around here he's known as a trader. But, actually, a total rascal.'

'Anna... anna!' protested the other.

'What, da?' retorted Thevar, contemptuously.

'Why must you break it all open in front of this thambi, anna!' remonstrated Sornavelu. To Chidambaram he said, 'So, you are going to set up a sugar mill?'

'Yes'

'Then, from now on sugar will be easily available.'

'You can set up a shop too!' said Thevar mockingly.

'Anna is like that only... and like that only he talks! The whole day long one will feel like listening to him talk like that only!'

'Stop pushing me in and out of that mouth of yours, I can't stand it! Step aside! We have to pass...'

'I myself have to go to your place, anna. Some bunches of bananas have ripened there, I hear.'

'But did you turn up all this while? No!'

'Anna, a Muslim trader called me to Needoor. It was supposed to be just a day's work – but it took all of four days!'

'Come quick then...we have to get going....'

'Right, anna!'

As they crossed the high street, Thevar remembered to ask how the new house was shaping up, and heard Chidambaram's detailed description with great delight. Regretfully he spoke of how his memory kept failing him these days.

Opening the bamboo wicket-gate, they went inside. The masons had not turned up yet; it was around the time they were expected. Impatiently they looked around. There was work to do in the grove.

Chidambaram observed, 'Looks like it's almost ready for the house entering, Mama.'

'We must see the priest about it and fix the date.'

A plantain frond swayed with the wind, flagging down a little across their line of vision.

'Mama, it seems bananas grow really well here!'

'Don't know what kind of soil it is, but bananas do thrive in this earth, thambi,' exclaimed Thevar, and went on to talk about different kinds of plantains and the many sub-varieties with great enthusiasm. Then he declared, 'After all, what's a banana tree, it's just like a woman!'

Chidambaram smiled.

'Everything else has a single month, a single season for fruition. But nothing like that for plantains and women!'

He was in a fine mood. When they emerged from the grove, Sornavelu was just coming in.

'Anna has sprouted wings! Anna is flying!' teased Sornavelu.

'Elei! You just mind your own business, da!' retorted Thevar, lengthening his stride.

Sornavelu eyed the plantain grove with its many great pendulous bunches of fruit. For two or three days there would be plenty of work to do. That made him very happy. Unfastening the sickle at his waist, he strode into the plantain thicket.

08 Chapter

SIVANANDI THEVAR STOOD facing the tamarind grove and looked beyond into the distance. There was a time when it had been part of a much larger natural formation. Then, it had been more like a forest than a plantation. He had himself seen it thrust its way little by little into the jungle and growing into it. The immense original copse of tamarind had fallen apart. It lay in fragments, a few trees here and a few trees there. How had this happened?

From the time he was five years old, he had gone often into the wild tamarind forest with his grandfather and father. At eight he had begun to climb the trees to shake down the ripe fruit. He was very good at it, too, leaping like a monkey from branch to branch, his grip firm on the branch as it swayed and dipped and sprang up again. One day in mid-leap, he had clutched at a rotten branch. It was a bad fall; he had spent a whole month in bed. Slowly the dislocated knee healed, and he could walk once again, but his tree-climbing came to an end.

Standing beneath the trees and surveying them from top to bottom, he would pick up the fallen pods and shake them to feel the loosening ripe seeds. Then he would send out a call for the harvesting. Those were the days when the grove grew tall as the sky, and the trees standing in an undergrowth of bush and twig were so dense that no man knew who stood next to him, as they shook down the fruit. Cleared of undergrowth now, the grove looked bare and bald. People could be seen striding along where one used to be afraid to walk.

Pazhani and Kaliyaperumal came up, dragging along some of the bushes and creepers that had been cut down on the previous day. Impressed and delighted at the magnitude of it all, Thevar burst out, 'You're not one bit like what I thought you were at first!'

Chidambaram shook his head modestly. 'What did I do? No work at all!' he said.

'Is that true? Just because you are the one to say it? One look at how much you have cleared tells the real story!'

Pazhani and Kaliyan came running up to them.

'So you came much earlier, did you?'

'A bit earlier, sir.'

'From now on, here is where we work. I have told the Chettiar.'

'The accountant told us, sir.'

Tying his vaitti securely between his loins, Thevar said,

'Give me some work to do, thambi.'

'Tell me, Mama,' said Chidambaram, giving him a steady respectful look.

'Me?' Thevar shook his head. 'Look here, thambi. I may have been born here. I have been going around this place for years. But nobody around here knows anything about all the things that you know! I am not saying it casually for the sake of saying it; I am speaking the truth. And why should anybody be ashamed to speak the truth, tell me?'

Chidambaram stood there in a deep silence.

'There are a lot of fellows here who talk smart, and boast about how there's nothing they don't know! Anyone who talks like that knows nothing at all!'

'True, Mama.'

'Seems Lord Sivan himself learned something from his own Son... it's there in the holy books, thambi.'

Chidambaram smiled softly.

'On the southern side, there's a lot of kaarai and kalli growing very thick, Mama.'

'It's a very old forest, that's why. Didn't sprout today or yesterday, did it? Has been around for so many years. And kaarai reeds, they're a peculiar plant...'

'...very difficult to cut down, indeed.'

'Tough as teak. Now, you handle the reeds. The boys can cut the aadathodai. As for myself,' Sivanandi pointed to the culms of towering tiger bamboo forking through the jungle from east to west. They were very ancient. Some were in full bloom and come to a final flowering before falling to the ground. Here where no humans walked, these gigantic culms had spread out as they pleased alongside a forest stream. Each thorn was of a marvellous size and length...

... Like a lion in the first flush of its golden-maned youth, the forest of giant golden-stemmed bamboos burst from the earth and seemed to stalk towards them. How could one even dream of hewing down this awesome bamboo and dragging it away! Around each clump was a twisting braid of briars. Every thorn would have to be sliced off separately before the stalks could be cut loose.

'Are you going to cut the thorns, Mama?'

'Yes, thambi.'

'Why not burn all this, Mama? Green shoots and all?'

'Look here, thambi, we need this bamboo! To build houses. To build the factory! Those briars will be good for building fences. Should we just drop all these plans and burn down everything? Tell me, thambi?'

'Oh...what you say is quite right, Mama.'

Sivanandi Thevar seized the hooked pole. What he could once accomplish with speed and vigour, as a strapping youth, long ago, was now impossible. What he had now was experience, and the knack of slicing and pulling off the thorns. Testing the edge of his sickle, Thevar went towards the bamboo thicket.

Hanging the hook on a convenient thorn, he brought

his palms together, meditated, and prayed to Mandhaiyya Thevar. To offer worship before beginning any work was the way things should be done. As though the chosen deity had given him permission, he gave himself a shake, and went on with it.

As the hook caught on the thorn, Thevar took two paces backwards, slashed twice and pulled. It frayed at the third slash. Slinging the hook on another fork, he dragged out the broken branch, but before it could fully emerge it got caught on another thorn. This was the difficulty in the bamboo jungle. One thorn would be entangled with five or six others. You had to cut at least ten or fifteen to get at the centre of the tangle before you could drag them all out. Invariably, until you had cleared the brambles all the way up to the height of two grown men one on top of the other, it would be harsh, tiresome work.

Advancing a little, Thevar slung his hook on the bamboo thorn by thorn, tearing them from each section of the stem and leaving them where they fell. The plan he had made when he first seized the hook was now completely altered. He dropped the idea of removing the briars and dragging the stems out of the clump. He had to weaken the bamboo culm as a whole, somehow. He had to isolate it. That was the first task at hand. Everything else would follow.

Thorn by thorn he slashed his way, and it became more and more frustrating. His arm throbbed. Leaving the hook hanging on a thorn, he climbed up a slope and turned his gaze to the southern corner. Chidambaram was not within sight.

He was struggling with the honeythorn.

The kaarai was covered in skeins of kovai and kurinja tendrils, and the clinging leafless 'lizard' vines. It seemed to Chidambaram that he would be drained of strength by the time he had cut them all away. They were only small creepers, but swarming from clump to clump, they had woven and plaited themselves around the reed-clumps and cactus beds and lay between them in a tight embrace.

Hacking at one clump to tear it loose, Chidambaram stumbled with the force of his effort and lost his balance. Thrown down, he rolled all the way to the bottom of the slope and lay there amid the reeds and the cactus.

The reeds stabbed him in the hips and legs. The flat blades of the chapatti-kalli cactus with their tiny bristles fastened themselves to his feet like leeches. Grabbing a low-hanging branch to pull himself up, he furiously tore at the chapatti-kalli and threw it away. The pain grew worse. There was a faint ooze of blood. He sat there, tired out.

Rising a little later and glancing around, he could not spot Pazhani, Kaliyan or Thevar. From the movement of the vegetation he guessed where they were. They wouldn't have seen him fall. The thought gave him some comfort.

A raging desire to avenge himself spurred him on. He flexed his arms and struck out with his sickle again and again, summoning up all his strength. And yet, defiantly the honeythorn stood rooted, a formidable enemy and every bit as cunning as he himself was. Even when it lost ground and lay rootless and supine, it stuck out in all directions, defying his touch. It was a dying warrior too proud to admit defeat.

Better an axe than the sickle, thought Chidambaram. It would make the job of chopping much simpler. Vanquishing the stubborn honeythorn might be done in much less time. But as luck would have it, there was no spot free of undergrowth where he could stand firm and wield the axe. No, it must be done with the sickle, arduous though that would be.

He heard Thevar call out to Pazhaniyandi. So! They were all quite close by, after all. As the boy's head bobbed into view, Thevar's elation at the successful completion of the tasks assigned by him expressed itself in a characteristically triumphant gesture: he swept his luxuriantly drooping whiskers back over his beaming cheeks. At Pazhani's answering call, he ordered, 'Go fetch the rest of your team! We have to make a pile of the thorns.'

When Kaliyaperumal turned up, they divided the work amongst themselves. Thevar paid no attention to their talk and arrangements, and continued to hack and pile up the bamboo. He had been labouring at it for a considerable time, sweat dripping from his body. He shifted the pole from one hand to the other.

A quarter portion of the first culm of bamboos had been destroyed, and now bore the distraught look of a plucked chicken. 'Tomorrow we can go right inside. Getting right into it means the whole culm will be wiped out,' he murmured to himself as he walked to the big punnai tree. He was too restless to sit down beneath it, though, and his eyes roved around in search of Chidambaram. Unable to spot him, he called out to him a couple of times. At the third call an answering shout rang back.

'Turn a little to the south, Mama, and come over here!'

'Can't see where, thambi.'

'Okay then, I'm just coming.'

Thrusting aside the sprawling shrubs and vines, Chidambaram finally emerged.

'What a jungle! I couldn't see you even though you were so close by!' said Thevar.

'For how many more days, Mama? Not long!'

'That's the way to talk! A few days more of this, and we'll be saying, 'Here there used to be kaarai, here there was bamboo, here iluppai. And here tamarind used to grow...' That's what it'll come to!'

Chidambaram listened happily, picturing it all. If, as Mama said, it all happened soon. But so far as he knew, deeds followed words at a many times slower pace. Every single step of any untiringly performed task was in itself the digesting and assimilation of many hundred thousands of words... And then here, where grass and weed and reed and tree had been, the outspread feathery crests of the sugarcane would rustle, and from the chimney of the sugar mill smoke would swirl up towards the heavens...

Their hearts full of hope, they walked together towards the banyan tree. This was one of two banyans in the forest, a gigantic tree with spreading aerial roots. The greenish black tendrils of a parasitic creeper wove in and out among them. Examining this puluruvi creeper, Chidambaram asked, 'What now, Mama?'

'First we cut the thorns, then the bamboos themselves. It will take a month, maybe a month and a half, to finish all this.'

'But if we both do it together, Mama?'

'It will be done quicker, true. But then won't the job of cutting down the kaarai come to a halt?'

'Yes.'

Wiping out the kaarai was as important from one angle as cutting down the bamboo was from another. That Thevar was supporting him, working shoulder to shoulder with him, gave him a fresh spurt of energy. Now it seemed to him that it didn't matter who joined in, or failed to. Each of the various tasks in the plan would proceed without impediment.

He discussed his plans with Thevar, who heartily approved of all of them. Every day they cut down the kaarai and made higher and higher stacks of it. Thevar and the two boys worked according to a fixed time – they came in the morning and left when it grew dark.

But to Chidambaram, the time of day or night didn't matter. He arrived every day and began work before the darkness had lifted.

As the work grew more exacting, his passion for it intensified. His whole life at present was totally entwined with the forest. He was bound and given over to it, in every way.

He would remain there even after darkness fell, toiling on in solitude, until an occasional hare scampered by or a pack of jackals sent up a howl. Then he would pause awhile, and watch the forest. As the days passed, it turned into a harsh testing ground.

Anxious that it would suck away his vigour, and leave him depleted, he began to whisper to it. To explain his purpose. 'Forest I haven't come to destroy you! I'm your friend! Lend a hand! Work with me!'

A swathe of the kaarai undergrowth had now been hacked away, leaving the ground bare. A straight path led into the bamboo culm, laying open its many mysteries and secrets. With the clearing of the kaarai, the date palms came into view. They were aswarm with golden scarab beetles, whose scintillating colours cast a spell over Chidambaram.

Meanwhile, Thevar's task of clearing the bamboo forest was not going as expected. It had been frequently interrupted, and had slowed down. Once he was away for twelve whole days purchasing cattle for the Chettiar. He couldn't resume work on the bamboos immediately on his return because he had to set off at once for Melur in response to a summons to attend a caste panchayat. On the third day after his return, Chidambaram came up to him.

He had finished clearing the entire tract of honeythorn.

In a transport of delight and pride Thevar flung open his arms and hugged him to his breast. 'In this whole world there is just nobody to beat Thambi at anything at all!' he exclaimed.

'Mama, the way you put in work, can anybody match you? Adeiyappa!'

'Even a lion grows old...won't it find its match?'

Chidambaram demurred at that, and said a lot of things that went straight to Thevar's heart. They went about their separate tasks. Chidambaram passed through the grove of bamboos and crossed over to the northern side.

Here was virgin ground, untouched by human feet. What wonders and marvels might be awaiting him here! But he had no time to speculate on them, or to discuss them with Thevar. He was as one possessed. What mattered most to him was the work he had taken on. Talk had indeed greatly reduced among these four men as they penetrated deeper and deeper into the forest, each in a different direction, each out of reach of any other human voice. The thrumming of cicadas and the humming of bees, bamboos fitfully creaking in the wind, the rustle of falling leaves, flowers dropping down, and the soft plop of fruit – this was all they heard, and this was their world.

Each day, Chidambaram was the first to enter the forest, well before dawn, as the birds were just leaving their nests. By the time Kaliyaperumal and Pazhaniyandi turned up he would have hewn down a couple of trees. Then Thevar would arrive. Nobody waited, though, for anybody else to come: each one of them had plenty to do, and there was no time to sit down and chat.

For confronting them was this huge jungle, and they were men in a frenzy to subdue it. To plant their flags upon its bared earth. For untold ages, beasts and birds had lived in this forest without human interference. Today, one meddlesome individual, a human being, had brought pandemonium down upon it. Tree and creeper, bush and bird, beetle and beast – all were going towards their extinction. A tranquil way of life had succumbed to the inevitable.

As Chidambaram advanced, monitor lizards and hares leaped out from the recesses of felled trees and lianas and made their escape. Monkeys sprang screeching from the trees and sped away. An amazing troop, there were more than thirty of them, big and small. Chidambaram gave them a wide berth, but a large monkey in the troop's rear bared its teeth and snarled at him. He had to duck behind a guava tree.

He discovered that in many ways the inner part of the forest was quite distinct. Here there were fewer creepers, and more shrubs. Flowers of many hues showered down their beauty, golden beetles darted up with a loud *jivvv!*, and tiny bees hummed incessantly. Hordes of dragonflies and butterflies flitted around.

Against the changing backdrop of the forest, he became aware, as though in a dream, that he was no longer chopping down vines and trees indiscriminately. Instead he was now advancing by carving a tunnel through the foliage. One day went by and then another, and he kept going on and on, into the darkness. No untrammelled vista opened up before him, as he had thought it would. Nothing.

It began to wear him out, both in mind and body.

After the fifth consecutive day of this toil, on his return home, he spoke of this to Thevar. Thevar pondered over it awhile. Then he grasped his hand and said, 'We ourselves have taken on this work, thambi... that's how it is!'

Ashamed at actually having itched to chuck it all up, he promised, 'I won't put down my sickle, Mama.' Greatly pleased, Thevar rejoined, 'We people are not like that, we are the Devendra Kulam! That's our tradition, thambi!'

And then Sivanandi Thevar told him all about how his clan had sprung from the King of the Gods, Indra himself. He described how Thevar society was transformed after the move from Madurai to the Thanjavur country, and how it became set in certain ways. Chidambaram heard it all, as though he were a child.

That night he couldn't sleep. Overcome in both mind and body by a restless excitement, he left the thinnai where he had fallen asleep, and walked through the dark lanes towards the jungle. It lay somnolent in the moonlight. Not a thing moved, not even the wind.

He climbed on the fallen trunk of a tree and looked intently around. In the moonlight the clumps of plants looked like little hillocks, and the trees like ropes hanging down from the sky. Drawing his sickle out from his waist-knot, he chopped down the bushes standing in his way and forged ahead for a while, until he had a feeling that he had lost his way. Here was a wilderness of cactus and pirandai vines.

There was no way through it.

Chidambaram retreated, climbed a poovarasu, jumped over to a punnai branch, and descended down a nettilingam. Coarse korai grass and rough naanal reeds grew in that spot. Low branches of poovarasu and wild guava had spread over the forest floor. Shoving them aside at every step, he went on. Birds shrieked in terror at the quiver and tremble of each leaf and branch. From time to time a sudden, heart-rending call broke out... He had heard such a cry in the daytime, and it had not bothered him. But now it gave him a piercing jolt.

Clambering up trees, springing from branch to branch,

retreating before the snarl of monkeys and the clamour of birds, Chidambaram advanced deeper into the forest. A silvery dawn had come into bud in the sky. From his perch on the pungai beech, Chidambaram's eyes widened at the view spread out before him. It was open ground, without a single tree, and no bushy mounds about. Leaping down he walked across it, traversing it from side to side. A rabbit sprang out from underfoot and raced away. A pair of jackals set up a howl.

Something stirred in a thicket.

Chidambaram stood silent, observing every little thing. An ox emerged from the clump, followed by another, and another. They were a bull and two heifers. Feral cattle, dedicated to the forest god Kathavarayan, they roamed free and had never submitted to any man. Many fruitless attempts had been made to capture them and tie them down. The one time that they had been caught, they broke their chains and simply ran away.

Crouching forward to conceal himself, Chidambaram reached a tree and scrambled up. Tails whirling, the cattle galloped around, the impact of their hooves setting the ground atremble. Cries and squeals of alarm broke out, foxes set up a sustained howling, monkeys screeched shrilly.

Chidambaram went back the way he had come, and when he told Thevar about it in the morning, the old man seized his hand and praised him, saying, 'Thambi isn't a fellow to be taken lightly!'

In the first part of the forest, the felled trees and vines lay as they were. Thevar took away just the malabar nut and the castor bushes, five cartloads of them. Nobody else came to collect anything for green manure. Unless the heaps of drying foliage were removed, there was no way to get the bamboo out.

In a low, persuasive tone of voice, Chidambaram carefully broached his plan to Thevar.

Thevar approved it.

'So then, when shall we set fire to it?' Chidambaram asked.

'Not tomorrow. A new month is born tomorrow... We'll do it next Friday, thambi.'

'All right, Mama.'

09 Chapter

SWIRLING CLOUDS TUMBLED over the sky, spilling a blurry darkness. A cold wind blew steady and calm. The sun had gone into hiding after blazing fiercely for a couple of days. People said that the rainy season had arrived earlier than usual.

Chidambaram and Thevar scanned the skies, flipped through the almanac, and decided after long deliberation that the incendiary plan set for Friday should be postponed. Until the masses of black clouds had dispersed and the sky grew pale once again, a fire could not be started in the forest.

Fed up of lounging around on the thinnai all day long and feeling smothered by the sheer tedium of it, he went to Panchavarnam's house at dusk. She received him with immoderate excitement and delight, but as he lay back on the cot, he felt drained of the very sensations that had so recently seethed within him. With Panchavarnam falling asleep on his breast, the night slowly wasted away to nothing.

'What's the matter with me? Mind and body are both desperate for something. It isn't for physical pleasure, for Panchavarnam is right here, snuggling against my chest... What is it that I want? What am I passionate about? What am I yearning for, so restlessly? I've come this far... but what for?'

His temples throbbed. His eyes hurt.

Gently he raised Panchavarnam and laid her back on the bed. Then he went outside. The wind held his body in a brief cold embrace and passed on. Wrapping a cloth around his head, he climbed the bank of the Vettaru, whose waters glimmered in the moonlight.

Slipping off his vaitti and leaving it on the embankment opposite the Pillaiyar temple, he descended into the warm flowing waters and took a bath. Twice he swam underwater from bank to bank, and when he clambered ashore he was shivering with cold. But his agitation had died down. He could feel a relaxed expression coming over his face.

It was bright daylight when he reached the grove, and many were on the road driving along heavily loaded oxwagons and pushing flat carts piled with sundried fish. The wind kept smacking the rainclouds and shoving them around. Standing under the punnai tree, Chidambaram surveyed the scene.

A red leech slithered along the blade of the shovel lying

near his feet, oozing foamy spittle.

The tools lay in an untidy scatter, sickle and hook, poles and axes and crowbar. He gathered them together under the guava tree and counted: a hooked pole and two sickles were missing. He couldn't recall where they had been kept. Thrusting through the thicket of kaarai, and the thumbai shrubs with their minute trumpet-like white blossoms, he searched until he found one of the sickles lying at the southern edge. The hooked pole hung from a jujube tree, but the larger of the two sickles was missing. Trampling the sparsely-leaved kaarai thorn-bushes and the thumbai shrubs all the way into the underbrush of stiffly-barbed cactus, Chidambaram returned empty-handed.

'Chhee, what a jungle this is... Can't find anything you put down! Dead beat, he sank down against the trunk of a palmyra.

'So this is where you were, thambi!' called Thevar, as he approached.

'Come, Mama.'

Thevar lowered his head and gave him a quizzical look. 'What is wrong with Thambi's health?'

With a shrug of his shoulders, he got up and said, 'Nothing at all, Mama...'

'Just now I went and saw Iyer...He says this year the rains will definitely come later.'

There was a pause.

'I'm wondering if we should start a fire at all, what with

the rains coming!' Chidambaram said at last.

Thevar made no answer to that. He was watching a dove fly out of a lightning-scarred tree. Chidambaram edged closer to him. 'Just look, Mama. Two sickles, three spades, and two hooked poles are missing!'

'Where could they go? Must be lying around somewhere here for sure...'

'Twice I have searched all over.'

'This isn't a small garden where you can find it quickly, is it? It's a huge forest, no?'

'That is true. So, I have an idea...'

'Tell me....'

'A small house, a hut... If we build something like that for keeping things, it will come in useful for so many things. We could sit down a bit, sometimes. And besides, the rainy season is almost here now...'

'It's a first-rate idea, but should we start building a house when the rains are about to come? Must think about it...'

'Not a pukka house! We need to plant just four bamboos and lay some thatch on top, that's all.'

Thevar listened.

He went on, after a pause: 'If there's heavy rain, or a strong wind, it'll fall down... So let it fall! Are we going to lose much by it, Mama?'

Thevar gave his nod.

Three days later, when the work was about to begin,

plans began to change. Each made certain alterations in the arrangements. The hut was now to come up a little beyond the iluppai, close to the jack tree. Thevar took on the task of digging up earth and trampling it down, with Pazhaniyandi fetching pots of water from the canal to moisten the clay. Kaliyaperumal carried the wet clay to Chidambaram, who piled and shaped it to make walls. Soon there was a wall about half a man's height on all four sides. Then Chidambaram took over the job of digging from Thevar. Digging deep gashes in the ground, he removed large quantities of earth. Work-hardened and experienced as Thevar was, it gladdened him to watch the skilful movement of Chidambaram's arms as they cut into the earth, picked up the clods and flung them down.

His spade struck a rock, and the ferrule slid off the handle, slipping it off. Exasperated, he turned to Thevar.

'Let it be, Thambi. We can fix it in a little while.'

'This is the third time, Mama!' declared Chidambaram, as he climbed out of the swampy pit he had dug.

'It happens when it hits something hard...And maybe it was already loose. Just have to beat it down again a bit, it'll be all right, thambi.'

'But Mama ... I've been watching! It never happened even once to you!'

Thevar smiled warmly at him. 'There was a jungle, thambi,' he began, 'where a rabbit and a tortoise were friends. They were great friends! One day they had a contest over who would run fastest to the farthest place within earshot! ...Why're you laughing, thambi? Because it's a strange contest? Isn't that it? Well, it's a very small story, just listen to the rest of it.'

'And so the race between the rabbit and the tortoise began. You don't have to ask how fast the rabbit was, do you? In just four bounds he had gone very-very far! Tortoise couldn't run at that speed, could it? So, slowly-slowly, it plodded on behind. Rabbit stood up on his hind legs and peered back to see where the tortoise was. But the tortoise was nowhere in sight. So the rabbit decided to take a little nap before the tortoise showed up, and squeezed himself under a thick clump of bushes. And when he opened his eyes, the tortoise had crossed the finish line...'

Chidambaram looked at Thevar with narrowed eyes. Winking at him, Thevar said, 'How do you like the story, thambi?'

'I don't like it at all!' retorted Chidambaram.

'It's a very good story!' insisted Thevar, as he tapped his spade on the ground and got up.

Day by day as the wall rose higher and higher, Thevar continued to instruct him on certain finer points. The thing with building a mud wall was that you couldn't build it very high until the base was thoroughly dry and firm. Chidambaram discovered that Thevar's objections had substance.

As the wall rose higher and higher, it began to sag at

one end. As Chidambaram slapped it into shape with the palm of his hand, Thevar climbed out of the clay pit and watched him in silence. Finally he said, 'You have improved a lot, thambi!'

'So, I have become a tortoise, is it!'

The other guffawed. 'Ho ho! You haven't forgotten that story?'

'That was a very good story, Mama!'

From between lowered lids, Thevar stared uneasily at him.

When the walls came up on all four sides, Chidambaram declared that another one needed to be erected across them on the inside in order to divide the house into two parts. Thevar didn't agree. It was his contention that it would detract from the spaciousness and the beauty of the whole edifice.

'But if we put up a barrier inside, there'll be one place to store things and another if anybody comes – for two people to sit down and chat a bit! To lie down a bit, Mama.'

'Mmm...'

'Over there, this is the way they build small-small huts, Mama.'

'Where… in Colombo?' enquired Thevar, shaking out his vaitti and retying it.

'Yes.'

'Oh...is that so?'

'When it is finished it will be really nice-looking,

Mama, really comfortable.'

Thevar merely smiled a taut smile... Deep down, he was fairly disgusted. How utterly cocksure Chidambaram was!

'This fellow shouldn't have been allowed to come too close. That is my mistake. That's why he dares to talk back to even me, face to face! But how can he keep quiet? He has four-five coins in his fist! That's why...'

They split up to do their separate tasks. Chidambaram set down a pile of grass and walked back, satisfied that things were working out the way he wanted. Thinking about Thevar, he grinned to himself. 'He's no tall coconut tree, just a naanal reed! Whichever way the wind blows, a naanal will bend!'

The very next moment he told himself that this was a despicable thought. For among all the men he had known, Thevar stood out for his acumen, his courage and his affectionate disposition. He believed in hard work. Of course, he was a little rough, too. But he had a sense of humour. And he was a real strong man for sure...

Chidambaram didn't know what it meant – this sudden insight.

Hearing the clinking of bells, he looked up to see a cart approaching the banyan tree. It was a neat spring-cart hung with bells and tassels.

'Namaskaranga!' said Chidambaram with folded hands.

'What brings you here?' enquired Chettiar.

'Heard the bells, came out to take a look, and here's our cart! Thought it must be you.'

'Good guess!' Chettiar said, alighting from the spring-cart.

'On your way home, sir?'

'Yes. So how's the work going?'

'Nothing to talk about.'

'Why? What's the matter?'

'No men, sir ...Can't seem to find the right kind.'

'Around here, that is a little difficult, certainly. I'm just going to Kuttalam. There should be some men on our in-laws' family farm. I'll see if I can arrange it.'

'That would be very helpful for me, sir.'

Chettiar grasped hold of the cart and went on, 'I'm also going to Kum'onam, I have a job to do there. Want anything done?'

'Nothing right now, sir!'

'Don't feel shy, just ask. Now we have all become one!'

'When you say this, do you know how it feels, sir!'

'I? What great thing have I said?'

With Chidambaram's warm unwavering look on him, Chettiar adjusted his uppercloth and murmured, 'So, then I'll take leave, shall I, Chidambaram?'

'Please come again, sir,' said Chidambaram courteously, bringing his palms together. Chettiar walked a few steps ahead and took his seat in the spring-cart.

'Sami!'

Chettiar turned. The voice was Chinnathambi Padaiyachi's. Out of breath with running, he stopped and just stood there, head bent.

'What is it, da?'

'I went up to the house, and Aachi told me you had only just left... When you go by Koranadu, please order three stones...'

'What for, da?'

'For her! She's gone...along with what she was carrying....'

Four days ago, Annakamu – seven months pregnant – had died of a five-day fever which quenched her breath forever. As soon as they heard the news, everybody dropped whatever they were doing and gathered at the house of bereavement. The wailing of women fell ceaselessly on the ears.

Chidambaram had watched the whole spectacle from under the boughs of a 'sleepyface' raintree, his glance shifting occasionally to the leaves as they drooped shut in the fading light. He was witnessing a death at close quarters after a very long time, and there were many things he couldn't understand. It was something quite out of his experience. He felt terribly stirred. When his mother died, everybody had gone off to work except the woman living opposite, and until they had all returned, the corpse had lain waiting.

But here the whole town had come together!

A little after midday, Annakamu's elder brother brought a new unwashed sari, a coarse red one from the loom in Chettiar's house. They said, that as Chettiar gave it to him, he broke into big shuddering sobs. It was he who had chosen her expensive wedding sari, a bright yellow one with a border of pandanus flowers. It had not even been a year and a half, and here he was now, presenting her with her last ever sari!

Chidambaram spent that entire day there, in the house of grief. Chettiar had come just a little in advance of the body being taken away, and Sambamurthi Iyer and Patanjali Shastri had also turned up. They stood for a while at a distance, and then left.

In the evening with the whole town assembled, weeping and sobbing, they took up the bier. Chidambaram helped carry the body up to the street of the Vellalas. It was quite heavy; he kept shifting it from time to time from one shoulder to the other.

Bells clinked once more as Chettiar's cart began to move. As Chinnathambi Padaiyachi stood there, with tears in his eyes, Chidambaram patted him on the shoulder, murmuring a parting word. Nodding, Chinnathambi wiped his eyes with his uppercloth.

They parted with no more words.

When Thevar returned home to lounge on the thinnai after his daily swig of toddy, Chidambaram set foot on the threshold. Thevar's face brightened at the sight of him. Wagging his head eagerly, he exclaimed, 'Come, come and sit down near me, thambi!'

He climbed on the thinnai and sat down.

'Where had Thambi gone all this time?'

'Just to the riverbank, Mama!'

'Thought you had gotten angry and gone off somewhere or the other!'

'Don't I know Mama's mind?'

'So you know a lot, do you? asked Thevar, beaming. 'Just now only I was telling Kunjamma that Thambi and I had a very big fight today!'

'Is ours really any kind of fight?'

Thevar sat up straight, and demanded, 'So what we had wasn't a fight?'

Chidambaram shook his head. Then he said, in a very low voice, 'Once in a while it seems to me, Mama.... that maybe what we have is the only real fight... What a fight really should be...'

Thevar did not reply to that. Instead, he called to Kunjamma, 'Thambi has come!'

The conversation coming thus to a sudden halt disconcerted him.

'Doesn't lose track of his thoughts, even if he's had a lot to drink!' he said to himself, as he went inside the house.

Three mornings later, when he reached the grove, Thevar was at the whetstone, sharpening a sickle till it shone. Next to him lay a bundle of soaked and dripping palm spathes.

'Was a bit tired, and just slept off, Mama.'

'What does it matter...?' answered the other.

'Where are the boys, Mama? Can't hear a sound!'

'They've gone to Pattu's house to fetch some fronds for the thatch.'

'So, that's why there's no noise,' Chidambaram untied the wiry lizard vine that he had used to secure the bundle of spathes and spread them out.

'They'll be here now,' said Thevar, taking up a spathe. With his foot, he held down the narrow woody casing as long as an arm, the outer cover of the bud in which the palm's flowers had once nestled. Then he began to rip it up lengthwise into thin strips of fibre. His hands raced over the work in amazing fashion. Chidambaram handed him spathe after spathe, after slicing off the tips and the ends. The tying of thatch with this fibre would be finished in a couple of days. It was no big task.

If the sky stays clear, we can start the fire tomorrow, he thought. The time seemed propitious.

Chapter 10

IN THAT EXTRAORDINARY forest, a little house was slowly taking shape. Together they had laboured over it, day after day. That it was their own creation gave them real pleasure. They collected the materials and tools that lay scattered in all directions, and sorted them into separate piles. Once that was done, there was no need to go wandering around looking for anything they needed, or stand around trying to remember where they had last put it. Every single thing had its own fixed place, and this became an unwritten rule among them.

One day, as Thevar sat on the cot chewing betel, Chidambaram brought in four scythes. Watching him impassively as he stored them carefully them under the cot, Thevar chuckled.

'What are you laughing for, Mama?'

'We already have such sharp sickles, as deadly as Yama himself, and here you are, coming in with these flimsy little swords! I couldn't help laughing out loud!'

Chidambaram did not offer an explanation just then that might have put the other's sceptical remark at rest. Instead he gave Thevar a probing look, musing to himself, 'Old fellow's a fox! Sly jackal knows a thing or two... and that's the cause of all his arrogance.'

He silently gazed down at his open palms. They had changed colour, and the skin had become calloused. You could pinch it again and again, with gritted teeth, and feel nothing at all. No sensation. That's how coarse it had become. The lines had disappeared under the whitened palm. This was the wealth earned through labour. As he felled tree after tree, his palms had seasoned like the timber itself.

Then he said calmly, 'It is true that if you chop down the trees with a sickle, they'll fall at once. But then see how quickly we get tired, Mama?'

Thevar shook his head. The explanation had not satisfied him. He turned away and walked off by himself.

Their joint trajectory had come up against a roadblock. Now he would go one way, and Thevar another. But their battle was not without dignity. It was a test of skill and wits, after all, with each man convinced that the path he had chosen was the right one, with no room to retreat or to sue for peace. And so, every day they returned home, their opinions greatly at odds, and their plans at cross-purposes. Now everything that happened between them began to take on a new meaning, and each dispute became the basis of another.

Until one day Thevar announced, 'Have to go to Neivilakku on urgent business; I'll be back soon,' only to stay away, apparently forever. Each day, every hour, Chidambaram awaited his return. The plan of setting the forest on fire kept getting postponed. With the rift remaining unhealed, Chidambaram began to see more clearly than before that his actions had hurt the older man's feelings.

It bothered him. Yet he consoled himself that what he was doing was along the right lines, and perfectly according to plan.

No use just sitting and waiting any longer, he thought, and got back to work. His gaze turning to the eastern corner of the forest crammed with noni mulberry and the tall kalli cactus, he decided it would be a suitable place to light the fire eventually – it would spread from the east in a northerly direction.

Four days after he had resumed work, Kaliyaperumal had to go to his village. He had been stubbornly refusing to go, but then his mother turned up, gave him a slap, and dragged him home. Silently Pazhaniyandi watched his friend leave. The next day he came alone to the forest.

Vast and overgrown as it was, it also looked ageless and untouched, a primeval wilderness. The two of them worked on to the shrilling of birds and the growling of animals, feeling no fatigue of any kind, making not the slightest complaint. One night, by moonlight, Chidambaram showed Pazhaniyandi the valley he had seen. Pazhani was so astonished by the sight that he couldn't figure out where exactly they were.

'Is this our place, sir?'

'Yes, it is,' nodded Chidambaram.

The other could scarcely believe it. They went around the whole valley, walking along the grassy bank, thrilling to the sensation of their feet sinking among the soft grass-blades. After mentally taking a measure of the spot, Chidambaram told himself, 'This will be the site for the sugar factory.'

The pandanus thickets divided the valley from the forest. 'If we go along the east bank of the Vettaru, we reach the jungle that hides the view of the grove of Saaya Vanam. A great big jungle, dark and gloomy and full of trees! Got to cut it down and clear it completely... There's no other way.'

They turned back and reached the hut. What were they going to do about the iluppais and the punnais? Pazhani had an idea: 'Let's burn down the iluppais too!' That appealed at once to Chidambaram. But it meant that they would have to work much harder than they had anticipated.

Towing along dried boughs and creepers, they walked from the northern to the southern side and then set them down between the trees. They couldn't make the trip southwards more than four times. Going through the pathless, tree-choked jungle was exhausting. This enemy's strength was mighty, they couldn't fight it any more.

They retreated northwards.

Pazhaniyandi lugged branches laden with leaves and tendrils and dropped them in the taazhai thicket. Clambering up a mulberry tree, he twined the swirling, flexible limbs on his pole- hook and flung them into the bamboo copse. For two whole days he kept at it, and by Sunday afternoon, it looked as though their plan would yield results.

Seizing Pazhani's hand, Chidambaram exclaimed warmly, 'You're an amazing boy!' Having such a thing said to him was a new and baffling experience for Pazhaniyandi. He gathered, however, that the boss was pleased with him.

'Come early tomorrow. *He* will be here... As soon as he comes, we have to start the fire.' Chidambaram said, his respectful tone making it clear who 'He' was.

'I'll be here, sir,' promised Pazhani, and took his leave.

Daybreak on Monday. Morning was a tender young thing, exquisite with the ceaseless trilling of birds and the humming of beetles. From somewhere came the splash of a tree toppling into water. Bamboos creaked. A solitary crow pheasant's distinctive call was followed by a flapping of wings.

Everything was almost ready. The time, too, seemed

just right: a cloudless sky, a dry wind without a trace of moisture. It would be easy to build a fire. The flames would swiftly shoot out and blaze away.

Chidambaram came out and shut the door. His gaze focused on Thevar approaching in the distance, alone, taking rapid strides.

'It's become all right again,' Chidambaram told himself and turned to look at the cane wilderness, full of tender green shoots. The cane had spread its curling vines over a vast area. Impossible to see where it began and where it ended. He loved cane. He longed passionately to cut it. Cane had brought prosperity into his life, and had made many things possible for him. Cane chairs and cots, and colourful baskets like those he had seen in the houses of the rich in Singapore... that was what he wanted for his own house.

Thrice he had tried to cut enough cane for his requirements, and although he had started out determined not to give up, he had had to retreat in disappointment every time. The cane stems were thickly entangled with one another, and whatever he cut couldn't be pulled out of the thicket.

When he had asked Thevar for ideas, he had laughed out loud and said, 'What big 'idea' do you need for this, thambi? Just put a little fire on top of its head, that's all!'

Chidambaram stared in silence at the cane. Its fate was sealed. There was no way to change that awesome verdict. The destruction of this part of the forest would be entrusted to fire!

Sickles and axes were already rapidly wiping out another part. It was not the bushes and creepers so much as the bamboos that were being brought down at a great speed. Nobody would have thought it would happen. Such immense bamboos, taller than one and a half or two coconut palms, shooting straight up, without a single crook or curve in them!

Ramapuram Mani Iyer took away four cartloads for the flour mill he was going to build, Natesa Shastri two cartloads for building a cattle-shed, Husain Saibu two cartloads for rebuilding his slaughterhouse. Cartload after cartload of bamboos was taken away, and yet no depletion seemed to have taken place at all. Around five hundred bamboos were still lying under the tall punnai tree.

His welcoming smile led Thevar to remark: 'So! Thambi is all ready!'

The two of them went up to the stretch of pandanus reeds. The preparations made by Chidambaram satisfied Thevar. 'We can start the fire right there, Mama,' he said. Thevar cast his eyes over the tract of pandanus screwpines. They extended southeast and disappeared into the cane. A fire started here would leap straight through the cane and burn it to cinders.

'Nothing that Thambi does can turn out wrong, can it?'

Chidambaram's smile broadened.

The wind swirled up, all of a sudden. 'It's blowing specially for us!' remarked Thevar, picking up the earthen fire-pot and walking ahead.

'Pazhani! Bring the palm fronds!' The boy leapt up, but Chidambaram stopped him and picked up the dried fronds and the hooked pole himself. Descending into the pandanus thicket, Thevar set down the pot, plucked sprigs of malabar nut and stuffed them in. The smouldering flame inside it flickered up in the breeze. Just come here and fan this flame, thambi,' instructed Thevar. Holding a broad dry frond with both hands, Chidambaram waved it expertly over the fire. Sparks rose up like streaks of lightning, vanishing in an instant.

Gazing in awestruck reverence at the flames, Thevar humbly removed his uppercloth and tied it around his waist. 'Mother Maari, Protector of the Poor! Mandhaiyya, Periya Karuppu...all of You! Stay by our side, support us! Protect us, and see that no harm befalls us!'

His eyes glistened. A glow suffused his face.

Ha!, roared the fire, sending a shudder through his body. He had received the expected command to feed it. 'Our god has said yes, thambi!' he exclaimed, picking up the fire-pot and entering the scrub jungle of upright taazham reeds. Finding a level spot, he set it down and piled dried palmyra branches upon it. The breeze died down. Gripping the dried base of a frond tightly, Chidambaram fanned the flames with all his strength.

Sparks shot forth and immediately turned to ashes.

'Come this side a little, thambi,' advised Thevar, and he switched directions, and stood there fanning away. The fire jumped to the green leaves, soared upwards and sprouted flames. Gathering up more fronds from the pile they had left to dry out, they threw it on the blaze, and it burst forth and leapt up with the wind's help.

Thevar thrust two fronds vertically into the centre. With a loud crackle, the fire ascended higher. He seized the burning fronds and hurled them into the forest of pandanus. They fell into the tazhai reeds, with their spathes of fragrant creamy-yellow blossoms...

'It's all burnt up!'

'Yes, Mama.'

'But even if one is all burnt up, another will catch fire.'

'Yes, Mama.'

Chidambaram forked up a flaming frond with the hooked pole and threw it into the conflagration. And the others followed, in turn, throwing frond after frond. The breeze returned, and shook the branches.

'The wind is blowing, thambi!'

'So it is, Mama ...'

'Our god is sending it!' exulted Thevar.

He nodded. Helped along by the wind, the fire devoured the leaf litter and rose straight up.

'Now we don't have to worry, do we, thambi?'

The fire did not fully take hold, but it wouldn't entirely die out either. Somewhere inside the wilderness it was smouldering on.

It caught the end of the pole, below the hook. Chidambaram had to stub it against the ground to put it out.

They couldn't stand near the honeythorns any more, for the fierce heat was like a slap in the face. Thevar drew a little way back and said, 'It has caught hold, thambi. To which Chidambaram concurred as usual with 'Aamaanga, so it has, mama!'

'Sokkappaanai pori!' cried Pazhani, clapping his hands in glee. The blaze had reminded him of the crackling and popping of rice kernels set in pots on bonfires during Karthigai, the winter festival of light and fire.

The three of them stood watching, their eyes darting and flickering with the rising flames bounding up from branch to branch, and following the sparks as they shot up to the sky, turned to ash, and fell to the ground. From the kaarai grass the fire vaulted up into the fresh green cane, the flames incinerating the tender leaves and sprigs, extending wave after fiery wave in the wind's wake.

This war was on two fronts – to the north-east the fire overran the taazhai reeds, while simultaneously, and diagonally opposite, it seized and burnt the bristly kaarai shrubs and the malabar nut. Red-hot flames overwhelmed the green, and took on the hues of the resplendent evening sky. The whole forest looked as though possessed by the fire. Carried by the force of the wind, the searing heat all but knocked them off their feet.

The three of them slowly returned to the hut. Even if the fire couldn't be wholly seen from between the trees, the smoke was visible as it rolled upwards, ball after unravelling ball.

For a long while Thevar observed its progress. Then he announced, 'Looks like it will burn for two days, thambi.'

'Two whole days, Mama?'

'Why do you ask?'

'Just like that...'

'Such a huge jungle! All of it has to burn up, hasn't it?'

'Aamaanga!'

A round smoke-ball emerged and went straight up into the sky, followed by fire-flecks scattering in all four directions.

'It's rising, it's rising! There...there!' they all cried.

A young palmyra's green fronds suddenly flared up. In a trice, the little tree with its spread-out halo of tousled leaves turned bald. There was no sign of the fire having come and gone, but the tree stood there...bald.

'Look, Mama, the green toddy-palm has burnt up!'

Sivanandi Thevar gave a nod of assent, adding, 'The fire hasn't yet really caught hold, thambi.'

Chidambaram gave him a mystified look. Pushing back his drooping cheek-whiskers, Thevar remarked, 'If the fire really takes hold, there won't be any smoke.'

'Is that so, Mama?'

'It is burning properly now only in the taazhai reeds...'

'Yesterday, I left eight taazhai flowers, thinking they're just buds, not ready to pick,' Pazhani said.

'Now they would have turned black!'

Pazhani didn't say anything. He was thinking of the large, long, fragrant blooms of the pandanus, nestling between the reed-like leaves...

'Let us just sit here a bit, thambi. Elei, Pazhani! Just drag that cot out here, da.'

They sat down on the cot and looked around the grove. The fire was indeed dying down, there was only smoke everywhere. Acrid black smoke!

'It's smoking.'

'No wind, that's why.'

'It's too green.'

'Not for a fire that's really caught on. Nothing cooks in it, it will all get burnt!'

'It caught on... now it is dying down!'

'It isn't dying down, it is smouldering and building up.'

'Really?' Chidambaram walked up towards the fire.

Heat fanned out from it. Foliage burned with a loud crackle. A monkey gave a horrible howl from overhead. He couldn't see where it was, in the smoke, but he could hear its staccato cries. A few steps ahead lay a pair of charred squirrels. The smell of their burnt flesh turned his stomach.

He blew his nose and walked on. A snake wriggled beneath his feet. For a moment he looked at it, and saw that it was a python, a large one.

Half its body had been grilled.

His flesh crept. Quickly he turned back. A monkey jumped down, with a cry. Another followed it, another, and yet another. As he watched, he found he couldn't count them. There must have been at least fifty monkeys. Even more, it seemed to him.

'The fire has started to work. But it is a big jungle!'

He suddenly thought of the wild cattle...Where would they be now? He kept thinking about it as he returned to the hut.

'So! What-all has thambi seen and found out?'

'Nothing at all, Mama,' said Chidambaram shortly, and sat down on the cot.

11 Chapter

THE NEXT DAY when they reached the forest, the fire was still spewing out smoke.

'So much smoke!' observed Chidambaram.

'It's burning deep inside.'

'But what if it just smoulders for many days, Mama?'

He laughed. 'For how many days can a fire burn low? After some time it has to flare up! And then it will burn really well!'

'Yes...'

They walked on for a while.

'Once the taazhai is wiped out, it will be one big job behind us.'

'That's right, Mama. It's huge, isn't it? Like some plantation...'

'A very old stretch of taazhai, thambi...'

'Taazhai clumps house snakes, don't they, Mama?'

'That's what they say, thambi. Even in the Mahabharatam there is a story about it. But you know, thambi, not once in my life have I seen any snake around here.'

'It must be there inside somewhere or the other.'

'Must be there,' agreed Thevar, his eyes probing the screwpine jungle. The fire had not fully taken hold and risen up but was circling close to the ground, overpowered by the black curtains of smoke fluttering towards the clouds.

The *chada-chada* of burning, sap-filled green trees was suddenly drowned by the howling of a jackal. At first, it sounded like just one, then two and soon it was many of them howling together!

'Foxes!' exclaimed Chidambaram.

'Yes...'

A pack of ten jackals ran past. The last was lame. Pazhani picked up a stone to hurl, but it hobbled away. 'Same foxes stole a little goat from the house of those people in the village, sir! The rich people who came over by ship.'

'Really?'

'Yes, sir! I used to work there...See that one with a limp? It was I who hit it! That night the moon was bright... if I had thrown one more stone, that jackal would have fallen down. But I couldn't find another stone...'

Thevar called him close, and gave him a pat. 'Real

champion, aren't you! Just like your father!'

'Shall we go that way a bit?' Thevar rose from the cot. Sending Pazhani home to have his meal, the two of them approached the thicket of cane, where the fire seemed to have subsided.

All of a sudden, flames shot up and pounced on the green fronds of the coconut, turning them into black cinders. It was speeding westward in a way they had never foreseen. Staring at it, Thevar spoke with feeling: 'Panchabhootham, they call them the five spirits, the elements. You can protect yourself against the wind, and against the rain. But fire? That's one element not one of us can escape from, thambi!'

'If there is a cyclone, or a flood, ten trees may fall but one or two will be left. But what's left at the touch of fire? Only ashes!'

'That's right! agreed Thevar. 'Ten years ago there was a fire, thambi, in the month of Thai. Eight days after Pongal, in the middle of the night, Balu Iyer's house caught fire. There was so much shouting and screaming. I had just lain down after coming back from the toddy shop...

'Thangam was there, then. She came running and told me, 'They are shouting in the agraharam! Go and see what is going on in that quarter, will you! The whole town is ablaze!'

'Came to the door and saw it was bright as day. And so much shouting, crying, talking... How could I just stand there? I ran out shouting to everyone, 'Elei! Brahmin quarter's up in flames, come quick!' Right behind me ran Annamalai – from the boat-people's household, and Patta Chellayya Thevar, Muruga Padaiyachi, Sankara Pillai, Narayana Pillai, we all gathered together, an army of us! Before we got there, the fire had already pounced on four-five houses in a row. There it was, that fire, burning away so freely and men and women were standing on the road and wailing *Ayyo Ayyo!*

'These Iyer people, they're a funny sort. They talk very fine about Vedas and Shastras and all. But when there is something that must be done, none of them comes forward! When this house caught fire, there was nobody to climb on top and put it out! Instead they kept shouting, one after the other, 'Call that fellow! Call this fellow!' It has always been like that with these people, from olden times! Like in that Ramayana story that these people always love to tell... a man's wife gets stolen by somebody, and instead of at once going after him and getting her back, he wants to get help-and-support from this person and that person!

'So I got terribly angry! Just couldn't bear it. Without even looking to see who was in front of me, I pushed them all away and shouted 'Elei, Annamalai, bring water, da!' and climbed atop the burning house. But he was nowhere to be seen in the crowd, he had gone into hiding somewhere. Sankara Pillai went right into the house and got four pots of water. He and Muruga Padaiyachi filled water again and again, and I took it from them again and again, and poured it over the fire. While on another side Patta Chellayya Thevar chopped green fronds and threw it into the fire. Poured more water. In the beginning it just hissed and hissed and disappeared, but we didn't give up. Kept throwing fronds and throwing water, by turns... In a while the whole town gathered there, from the agraharam right up to the river, in a line of men and women handing pot after pot up to us, and that's how we put out the fire. Ten cattle, one child...couldn't count how many sets of pots and pans...all burnt up. Just imagine, thambi!'

'That's how it is, with fire. One time in Ceylon, about a hundred or hundred-fifty huts were completely razed down. It happened in the blink of an eye. At least there was water within reach to put out that fire. Nothing like that over there! If something burns, it has to go out by itself. In that fire accident, ten children and three women, and two men got completely burnt and died.'

'That's how it is, thambi. Here we are, looking at this fire, and then it burns a whole house, and a tree full of green leaves.'

'Before I left to come here, there was an accident. In a trice, four houses and eight shops were burnt up...all gone...'

'You think that is something, thambi? Two years ago, right here, our temple car caught fire!'

'The chariot?'

'Yes... it returned to its place after the temple procession, and the next morning it caught fire.'

'How could that happen? Sounds very strange!'

'Some fellow stuck the pot of coals in between the railings and went off. All night long the embers smouldered, and at dawn it caught fire.'

'Is it the same chariot that is there now?'

'Yes. We straightened it out here and there and made it all right. Now you won't be able to make out much, thambi.'

Watching the fire spew smoke-curls, Chidambaram declared, 'Nobody can be sure about fire!'

'Once the main street of our village caught fire. We thought it would spread to the north, and threw water on it, cut green fronds and threw them in, too, but then a wind turned up and the fire went southwards.'

'This fire it must not spread like that.'

'Why should it? Is there any house here? Any place where people live? Over there are tamarind trees, and beyond are fields. Fire won't reach that far... But as you say, there is nothing greater than fire.'

The fire that had been roaring thus far, slowly subsided. Whatever they had both anticipated had not taken place. Burnt leaves crackling underfoot, they approached the fire. The flaming limbs of trees were turning into fiery stumps. What an incandescence! What majesty there was in this conflagration! The glowering, radiating heat made it unapproachable.

'The fire must have gone and fallen deep inside.'

'Yes'

'It may take four days to burn up.'

'Four days?' repeated Chidambaram, surveying the forest. He had to admit that the smoke-filled expanse of honeythorn and pandanus amply bore out Thevar's estimate. But would the fire restrict itself to a small circumference, as they had expected, and then burn itself out? Or would it grow unfettered? Like a holocaust at aeon's end, would it sweep over the forest and beyond it, reducing the fields and pastures to cinders? And would it reach the orchard of jack trees? It was hard to say for certain.

'As long as everything ends up well, that's enough, Mama.'

'Yes, thambi...'

A pack of jackals went howling past the tamarinds and disappeared behind them. Birds flapped confusedly around in the sky.

'It's the heat... the force of it is driving out the birds!'

'Such heat, can't even stand here!'

He drew back. 'The sun's overhead, shall we go and eat, thambi?'

'Looks like it will be good if somebody stays here, Mama.'

'Where's the boy?'

'He's just gone to have his food ...'

'Then he'll be coming back now. I'll go and see Sambamurthi Iyer. Come over to the house when you go back home.'

'Anything special?'

'You know we have a girl of marriageable age in the house. There's news that people are coming from Villiyanoor to have a look at her. It is not certain. But in any case, it's better we stay in the house.'

'Yes, I will also come soon.'

He saw Thevar off and went and sat down on the string-cot. The entire sky was covered with black and white smoke. Emitting shrieks of terror, birds and animals were flitting and scampering about. Consuming everything in its grasp, the fire surged on.

A crow flapped its wings and blindly fell across Chidambaram's cot, startling him. Seeing what it was, he gave a sudden grin of relief. Something made him seize it by the feet and hurl it in the direction of the flames. Watching the crow fall unresistingly, and without a sound, he had an urge to watch its wings blacken and turn to ashes. Heedless of the blazing heat, he went forward with the pole and speared the burning crow, raising it aloft.

The stench made him wince. He pushed it back, deep into the fire. Trying to withdraw the pole, he found it was burning steadily. This was the second of the two hooked poles, the one with a curved sickle tied to it, and it was crumbling to ashes around the sickle. He stared fixedly at it...

Moral codes. Life. A strange thought came to him about the futile search for meaning. Sweat broke out all over his body. He staggered. In a frenzy, he flung the pole into the flames and sank down on the cot.

The fire leapt noisily up and assaulted the punnai, leaping from leaf to branch to trunk. Watching it billowing, he felt its ferocity work something extraordinary over him. It was churning him up... He was losing his balance... At this rate, what would happen to him?

The fire stopped flickering from branch to branch of the punnai, and began to burn more powerfully. He could no longer sit on the cot; the wind was throwing the heat right at his face. He wiped his face with his towel and got up just as Pazhaniyandi arrived.

'Elder sister had come from the village, sir. So I got late.'

'Your own akka?'

'Yes, sir... Headman's people say you must come quick.'

'Who said?'

'The lady.'

'Stay here and take care of everything, I'll just be back.'

'Right, sir.'

'Don't go near the fire to watch the fun!'

'No, sir.'

'Careful, the fire is very strong, you stay far away, I shall be back soon.'

'Two seasons I've walked on fire, sir...!'

Chidambaram paused in mid-step and looked back at the boy. So here was one who had stepped over live coals at the temple festival...

But he didn't ask him about it.

When he crossed the grove and reached the road, the village watchman asked, 'Looks like you have started a fire?'

'Yes.'

'As far as I can see, there is only smoke!'

'Really?'

'Yes.'

'Fire hasn't caught on yet.'

'It's not a small garden, is it, to catch fire just like that? It's a forest, no?' the man chuckled. 'Iyer said for you to come and see him once.'

'I want to make the trip too. But one by one this or that work comes up and it keeps getting postponed.'

'A thousand jobs you have been doing all alone!'

'What jobs! Everything is just lying around just like that, nothing is finished...'

'How can that be, for haven't you have cleared three fourths of this grove all by yourself in just a bit of time, haven't you?'

'I need four men to drive a cart,' disclosed Chidambaram.

'Nobody to drive a cart properly in this place. But anyhow, just go and see Ponnuvelu Thevar, he will arrange something or other. But there's one thing: people around here are the kind who plant crops, they won't leave it and do some other work.'

'When there's nothing to do in the fields, why not do some other work?'

'How can they do that?' countered the watchman.

To Chidambaram it looked as though the whole social structure of the village was a knotty tangle that defied all reason. As though in confirmation, an incident that had taken place twelve days earlier now branched out in his mind.

Having said he would come to work on Monday, Annamalai had laid down his scythe, turning up in the morning to announce 'Our Chettiar says there is a tree that has got to be cut down at his place. Only after finishing that work can I do your job, sir.'

Fixing him with a pointed look, Chidambaram demanded, 'How much coolie will he give you?'

'What coolie-voolie, sir! For four generations we have been working at his place. The land our huts stand on, the food we eat, this cloth around the body... Everything is his, sir.'

'Hmm.'

'Look here, sir, it's been more than thirty years since

Chettiar came to that grove of his. Is the jack tree giving any fruit? Is the mango? The coconut? That gentleman doesn't know a thing about all that, it's all whatever we see and tell him.'

'Strange!'

'So, he is like that only...But what about our Aachi? Chettiar's lady is even more like that. Talk about a virtuous lady – that's just what she is. Doesn't even tread hard on the earth once, or speak a single word in anger, does Aachi! If I pluck some fine peethar mangoes and take them up to the house, she'll first ask, 'Ei'nda, did you take some for yourself?' Even as I stand there mute, she'll always say, 'How many times must you be told – only after you take is the rest for us!' She is a girl from a very great house, and the house she has come to is also of that type. It was only for that family, for the first time ever, that special bridal saris were woven here. It was the talk of the whole town! From Kasi, from Rameswaram, from all those places, they would send people over here for bridal saris. It was only because of this family that another Chettiar started to weave saris here....'

'When are you coming back to work?' cut in Chidambaram, tired of his talk.

'Soon as I finish there, sir.'

'When will it finish?'

'Five-six days, sir!' he declared, shouldered his scythe and went off.

And didn't turn up for eight days.

Chidambaram told Thevar about him.

'You know, that fellow is completely crazy. He likes to stretch himself out as though he can do everything – head in one place, feet in another. I will tell the Chettiar and drag him here by the tuft!' promised Thevar.

Chapter 12

AFTER IT HAD spat out smoke for four days, the fire smouldering in the heart of the jungle interior suddenly burst into a mighty blaze and spread in all directions. His schemes and calculations were caving in. Sunk in silence, eyes delving deep into the burning forest, Chidambaram watched the flames pounce like forked lightning and race over it. Caught upon red-hot tongues, its cool green was being scorched black.

It was a holocaust. The very picture of doomsday. Over the immense primordial forest raged a sea of fire. Having devastated the cane thicket and the pandanus clumps, it reduced the new house he had built to ashes, and leapt to the tamarinds.

He stood watching the conflagration from the bank of the stream until he was beaten back by a blast of heat. Sivanandi Thevar approached from opposite, clambering up knolls and down hollows. Setting eyes on the wildfire, he stood transfixed. For a long moment he said nothing.

His silence troubled Chidambaram.

'What is it, Mama?'

'Now, if there isn't any wind, it would be a good thing.'

'That's true!' he agreed, nodding vigorously.

But the wind which had so far been decorous now stepped up its tempo. Trees bowed and swayed, their fire-laden branches swinging this way and that. With a shrill scream it pierced through the conflagration and sped on. Rising and falling in billows like ocean breakers, it slammed itself against the trees.

A wind was all right if it blew moderately for a few days. But now wildfire and wildwind together threatened to finish off everything in a single day. Everything. Chidambaram bit his lip worriedly, surveying the scene.

'Will it rain, Mama?' he asked.

Thevar looked up at the sky, and turned to him.

'Rain?' The question hovered in the air.

If the wind kept on like this, the fire might go on raging for many days. Every tree, every blade of grass, every herb would be utterly scorched. The last trees were the iluppais, the oilnuts. Once those oilnuts burned down, the clearing of the forest would be complete.

It would become open ground.

All of a sudden, the next day, the wind stopped as though it had simply sunk into the earth. Not a bough moved, not one creeper or leaf-cluster. Everything stood still, waiting.

A greenish darkness spread over the reddened sky.

'It's raining in the east, thambi,' Thevar announced, scanning the horizon.

'Will it come here?'

'Looks like it!'

It did not rain. The darkening sky now turned pale, and the black clouds moved eastward. But the wind did not start up again, and the towering flames had diminished to sparks. The fire now burned quietly, its fury abated. They went home, thinking it was all out of their hands now, and feeling wretched about it.

Walking on ahead of Chidambaram, Thevar stopped and turned for a moment, to say, 'If you really think about it, thambi, there is nothing greater than fire.'

Chidambaram said nothing.

'Like that monkey who burned down Lanka. That is how it has happened right here, isn't it?'

'The hut we built is gone.'

'Everything is gone, thambi!'

A wrenching sense of loss oppressed them both. But Chidambaram would not acknowledge his guilt even to himself. The way he saw it, it was true that despite his efforts some things had gone awry with his plan. But that was all.

The next day they were forced to remain on the canal-bank, beaten back by the fire's hot breath. The tamarind trees had all burned down. They stood there in a bald black row, without a single limb. The punnai and the banyan to the south were still burning.

On the twelfth day of the fire, it seemed to be appreciably weakening. Like a tortoise withdrawing into a shell, the combustion contracted and concealed itself. They crossed the canal and came to the forest's edge. The fire was still flickering inside, and entering it was impossible. Until the embers were utterly extinguished, it just could not be done. And it was hard to say when it would really die down, because it was not just a part of it, but the entire forest that had caught fire. Every day they would come and stand at the edge to watch the fire. As though it were some kind of spectacle. It became a habit with them.

More than Chidambaram, it was Thevar who wilted under the strain. His liveliness and banter were greatly reduced. His dejection worried the younger man.

'Nothing is in our hands, Mama!' he said, by way of consolation. Thevar turned slowly, pushed back those great drooping moustaches of his, but no word came from his lips.

Quite unexpectedly, the rain did arrive one day. They were so happy that they almost couldn't bear it. Throwing his towel down on the thinnai, Chidambaram came out and stood in front of the house, letting himself get thoroughly drenched. 'Plenty of rain, Mama!' he called out.

'Yes, even if it has come a little late, it is a good amount of rain, thambi!'

'Adeiyappa! How hard it is pouring! Looks like it will rain for two days, Mama!'

'Why are you getting wet, thambi? Come inside!' said Sivanandi Thevar, wiping the raindrops from his forehead and returning to the thinnai.

'Fire will completely go out now. Even if it did come late, the rain has come in torrents!'

'If it had come just four days earlier, that would have been very good!'

'It is doing at least this much for us, Mama,' said Chidambaram, leaning back against the thinnai. The sky continued to darken as minutes passed, and as a portent of a massive downpour, the wind stopped.

'There's no lightning at all. Or even thunder, Mama!'

'Just plenty of rain!'

'The fire too began slowly that day, just like this. The rain is also doing the same thing.'

'As they say, *Mazhaiyum magapperum mahadevanukku thaan theriyum!* The time of rain, the time of birth – only the Great God knows.

Chidambaram smiled.

'One season five years ago, there was no rain. Absolutely no rain! For seven months the sun blazed as though it were the summer month of Chittirai. Crops all withered and turned black. No water even for the goats and cows, every pond and pool had dried up completely. Not one god we left out of our prayers, there wasn't a pujai we didn't perform. That whole year passed without a drop of rain.'

'Really?'

'Yes...'

'How heavily it pours now!'

'Yes, I can feel the spray right here. Just roll down that screen, and come and sit here.'

He untied the bamboo screen and pulled it down to shield the thinnai from the slanting rain. Thevar settled himself comfortably against the pillar opposite him, and began:

'Do you know this story, thambi? ...Once, the gods and the demons churned up the Ocean of Milk to get the nectar of immortality. The gods ate up all that amudham without giving the demons even a drop. And that was it: they lost their minds! Began to think there was nobody greater than them in the whole world, that there was nothing above them! Brahma took one look at them and could stand it no more. Their arrogance was atrocious, they were all swollen up with it. 'Ada, you stupid gods! Am I not above you?' he said, and then he hung a light up in the sky.

'There it was, that light up in the heavens. Something that had never been there before. So new and shining bright! The gods didn't know what it was, nor did the demons, nor did anyone else on earth. The gods huddled together and thought about it. Added and subtracted, made calculations. Even then they couldn't figure it out.

Finally they sent Agni to take a close look. So Agni zoomed up, and up, but he couldn't go close at all. It was spewing flames, too, ten times, a hundred times more flame than the God of Fire himself. And so, from a respectable distance Agni called out, 'Oh Light! Who are you?'

'The Light retorted, 'Never mind who I am. Who are you?'

'And Agni declared, 'I am Agni! I am Fire. I can turn everything in the entire world into ashes if I want.'

'The Light gave a laugh. 'All right then, just turn this to ashes!' it said, and plucked a blade of grass and flung it down.

'Agni was furious. 'As though I can't burn this miserable wisp!' he snapped, and applied his whole strength to the job, determined to turn it into ash in a second. Mm-hmm nothing doing! Not even a tiny bit of that wisp caught fire!'

Kunjamma brought a platter full of popped maize kernels.

'Have some, thambi.'

'What about you...?'

'Me?' repeated Thevar, and began to pound betel leaves for a chew.

Tossing a few kernels into his mouth, Chidambaram went on: 'The fire must have completely gone out by now, isn't it, Mama?'

'Must have turned to ashes and mixed with the running stream, thambi.'

That evening it rained a little less. Thevar rolled up the bamboo screen and tied it up under the eaves. People were going about on the street, covering their heads with gunnysacks. Here and there were umbrellas made of pandanus fronds, and bamboo rain-hats. Thevar crossed the thinnai and called out: 'Ramu! Have the fish come out of the pond?'

'Yes, Mama!'

'Pond is flooded!' exclaimed Thevar, grabbing an umbrella and going out into the street. It was ankle-deep in rushing water. He could see 'scorpion' fish and catfish. If it rained any more, and the pond broke its banks, the eels and the carp, and those other strange black 'walking' catfish, the panai-eris which could slither up toddy palms, would all come tumbling out, shoal after shoal, struggling against the current.

This was a fine time to fish! Everybody loved this after-monsoon pastime. They stuck conical cane hats on their heads, seized hack-knives and plunged into the flowing stream to hunt out the fish. The storm had died down to a thin drizzle. Chidambaram stepped into the street aswarm with people. Men, women and children were splashing and jumping about, slaughtering the fish and piling them up in heaps. 'Do the fish always come out like this, when it rains a lot?' he asked.

'Yes, when the pond breaks its banks,' replied Thevar.

'Really!' he marvelled.

'Come, thambi, let's go take a look at the grove.'

Pushing away a fish that had leapt out of the water and fallen at his feet, Chidambaram asked, 'The fire must have burnt out by now, don't you think, Mama?'

'What do you think?' Thevar's laugh was a low growl of triumph.

They reached the street of the Vellala farmers, which overlooked their fields. Beyond the forest was dimly visible. Fire-scorched, rain-ravaged, it looked desolate. A vista of emptiness.

On the slippery embankment of the fields, Chidambaram was about to lose his foothold when Thevar gave him a hand and pulled him up.

'No hurry, thambi, walk carefully,' he advised and so Chidambaram let him lead the way. Walking in the wet, grassy earth between the blackthorn trees lining the fields was difficult. The slush was sticky and clung to the feet. Yet he did not feel like cursing the rain. It had solved one of his problems, after all. Inaccessible till yesterday, the dense and intractable forest was now admitting them in.

But Thevar was aghast at what had happened to the jungle. He could never have imagined such a transformation. Agitation contorting his face, he kept pulling at his whiskers and thrusting them back, exclaiming again and again that all his hopes and schemes had been belied.

'There is not a single tree in this place, thambi!'

'Yes...'

'We didn't know it would happen like this! It's all gone!'

Chidambaram went into the scorched and rain-battered hut. It was an utter ruin. The bamboo poles that had held up the walls, and the walls themselves, had all caved in and gone back to the earth. Everything that he had collected and kept there – his entire wealth in the form of tools – had been washed away.

Thevar went up close to Chidambaram. Lowering his pandanus frond umbrella, he asked, 'Thambi, you didn't by any chance keep any cash here, did you?'

'No.'

'It has all happened differently from what we thought.'

To comfort him, Chidambaram smiled a small smile and said, 'But even that might work out to our benefit.'

The other nodded vaguely.

Feet sinking into the heaps of sodden ash, they walked around the forest. Trees that had taken many days to bring down had been burnt to cinders. What the fire had done defied the imagination. Awesome in its intensity, it was now becalmed, shrunk to nothing.

They came to the tamarind trees. Charred and beheaded, they looked like crude black lines scrawled over the sombre sky. Sivanandi Thevar raised his eyes to the trunks, bereft of branches. Then he moved slightly backwards, as though recoiling from the sight.

The ground had been cut away from under a whole

way of life. Never again would any long pole hook itself on any tamarind branch here, and shake down the pods. The last of the pole-hooks had already done its work last year. Who knew who had cast the evil eye on this sacred duty he had inherited as head of his family! It was all over, finished.

He couldn't bear to stand there any longer on this field where he had been so utterly routed. As he strode away, Chidambaram hurried behind, asking, 'What is it, Mama?'

'There will be no more puli!'

'Why?'

'Trees are gone!'

'So what if these trees are gone, Mama? Can't tamarind be bought from other places?'

'Of course, we can buy cartloads and cartloads. But will it ever be like the puli on our own trees, thambi!'

There was a pause, before he went on, 'We'll have to drive our carts through village after village. One fellow will say there is tamarind, another will say there is none. And is that all? Will we ever get the kind we want? The quality? That we'll have to see...'

Puli. Tamarind. What was it, except a thing to flavour kuzhambu with? Could its sour tang ever compare with what would replace this wild grove – orderly fields yielding cash crops of sweet sugarcane? To Chidambaram, social bonding built on trivial eating preferences made no sense. This way of life seemed very remote, it would never really connect with him. His own self mattered. That was what was important. This sense of his own separate existence was life itself. 'I! Only I! Myself!' he repeated to himself, secretly, as though reassuring himself of this inner reality.

Yet those tamarind trees thrust themselves through the words into his consciousness. Turning to Thevar, he said defensively, 'We didn't burn them down on purpose!'

'But I never blamed you!'

They walked from the southern tip to the northern part of the forest. At first it looked as though the fire had not extended its sway entirely over this area. All they saw were seven or eight trees that had lost their foliage.

Then, under an iluppai tree, lay a charred heap. Kathavarayan's bull! He stared at it, shaken. This broiled carcass had once been a majestic emblem of the guardian deity. This animal had reigned supreme over the dark jungle, and now it lay dead.

Thevar looked this way and that, whispering, 'The fire didn't spare even Lord Kathavarayan's mount!'

'Nothing it touched could escape, Mama.'

They walked on. A little way ahead lay a cow and calf, baked alive in the fire. Not just trees and plants, but every form of life caught in the conflagration had been scorched and shrivelled to cinders. What they had felt when they saw the wreckage of the hut they had built, and the razing of the trees they had felled, was more than matched by the grief that gnawed at their hearts at the sight of these dead cattle. Yet it was a grief that could not be shared. It took a different form on the minds of each. Unable to make conversation, they walked on in silence, slowly.

They reached the summit of a mound. Sensing the subtle upheavals in his companion's mind, Chidambaram ventured to say, 'Whatever has happened has happened, Mama. We can't go on thinking about what is lost. Profit or loss, now our work has become easier, hasn't it?'

The other nodded, and then added sadly, 'But to lose those bamboos and those tamarinds makes my heart so sore, thambi, it cannot heal!'

'I am also feeling very bad about it, Mama. How much trouble you took! You sweated blood, cutting down those bamboos! All by yourself, you brought down this great big invincible forest...But see what happened in the end. It has all turned to ashes...'

'That is what it means to be human. Some Force that a man's brain can never reach is always, always knocking him down, rolling him down...'

'And yet, Mama, we won't allow ourselves to get worn out!'

Thevar nodded. 'That is not in our blood!'

'Yes, Mama, that is what is special.'

As they traversed the hillock heaped with ashes, Chidambaram drew pictures of the future in his mind: where the house would stand, where the sugarcane would be stacked to feed into the mill, where the jaggery ought to be stored. He made mental notes of everything.

'So, then, thambi! When is the work going to start?'

'When?' repeated Chidambaram. 'You are asking me 'when', Mama? If only we get the workers, we start right away!'

'That's good, thambi!'

'In any case we need workers. And it doesn't seem like we can get the right sort of men around here. So my idea is to go to other places and find some workers... what do you think, Mama?'

'Ten-fifteen years ago, we did get workers from outside for some temple work here.'

'Sambamurthi Iyer and Kanakasabai Chettiar said they would send some of their fellows. But will that sort of arrangement be convenient? We have to think of that!'

'A woman cannot have two men at the same time, thambi!'

Chidambaram laughed out loud.

'You can bring back the workers we need in just ten days.'

'That's what I think, too, Mama. If they come, they will need huts to live in.'

'By the time you come back, I will arrange something, thambi.'

'Then I'll leave tomorrow.'

'Right.'

The huts had to be built and ready before any workers arrived. Before that, the half-burnt timber had to be hauled away from the site. For the building itself, there was no bamboo at all. The enormous copse of giant bamboos was all gone. Would he who had supplied cartloads of bamboo to so many people now have to drive his cart around in search of bamboo?

This job, however, he entrusted to Thevar. The man knew the intricacies of such dealings. Wherever bamboo was to be had, he would find it and bring it here.

When they reached the road, Chidambaram smoothed down his ruffled crop of hair and said, 'Please Mama, come let's go and meet Iyer.'

'No, thambi, where is the need? I'm going to meet Stonehouse Chettiar.'

'So, the bamboo splits have been fixed already, have they, Mama?'

'Tomorrow they will lay the tiles. If you go that side, just come home, thambi. For many days you have completely forgotten our house!'

'Well, but then, you are here with me, Mama!'

'Oho! So that's it!' Thevar clapped his hands together and laughed heartily. 'How well you talk, thambi!'

'I? You mean me, Mama?'

'Who else am I talking about?' Thevar rejoined. Chidambaram grinned at him, and set off to see Sambamurthi Iyer. As he neared the brahmin quarter, he began to wonder if he would find Iyer at home.

'Let him not be there,' he wished. A thrill of energy

racing through him, he braced his arms and twisted them behind his back as he strode along.

Padmavathi stood at the door.

'Isn't Sami here?' he asked, carefully addressing Iyer in the fashion prescribed for a brahmin gentleman.

'No,' she answered shortly.

'Good thing, too!' he thought to himself, seating himself comfortably on the thinnai. Padmavathi knitted her brows and gave him a stare. Then she swiftly turned and disappeared indoors.

She'll come back, he thought. She will come

He sat there for quite a long time, but didn't catch a glimpse of so much as her shadow. Irritation mounted in him as he sat on, examining the contents of his loosened money-belt. Finally he jumped off the thinnai and began to walk away very fast.

...Now it was Panchavarnam he was thinking about. As soon as he stepped into her house, Sundaravadivu ran to welcome him.

'After that day, we haven't seen you at all!' exclaimed Panchavarnam.

'Had some work to do.'

He went inside and lounged on the bed.

'Everybody around here is saying you are going to set up a sugar mill,' Panchavarnam said, sitting down beside him.

He grabbed her hands and pulled her close.

'This lord can't wait even a little bit!' she cooed, as he kissed her on the forehead.

'That work of building the factory, how goes it?'

'Don't ask me anything about the factory!' he retorted.

She gave him a keen look, and a fond smile. Then she sank her head into his lap.

'Wherever I go, it's the same thing they keep asking. Can't stand it!'

Raising her arm, she stroked his back.

'You don't think of me at all, did you!'

'Is that why I have come now, then?' he retorted.

'Oh, you think so much of me! I can see that!' she mocked.

There was a soft rap on the door.

'Panchu... The mirasidar...'

She sprang up, exclaiming, 'The old dog of a landlord has come! To take the life out of me today as well!'

Chidambaram gently raised her face and kissed her on the lips. 'What...?'

'Dasi...that is our caste.'

'Mm...?'

'Please come tomorrow.' Leaning against his breast, she sobbed, tears trickling from her eyes.

After she left him, he thought about it. 'Why did she cry?' He could make no sense of her caste-decreed duties and obligations. Nor of her tears.

Opening the door, he left the house by the back door.

The sky was utterly clear. The moon shone. A cool breeze blew.

He walked on until he reached the Kaveri. Entering the water, he bathed for a very long time.

Chapter 13

FOR FOUR DAYS after Chidambaram left, Thevar worked according to the plan they had made together, without pause. Pazhaniyandi toiled willingly under his directions, wholly to his satisfaction, and soon the half-burnt timber had been hauled to the riverbank and piled up. They also built four huts for the workers. On the eighth day they laid the thatch for the roofs. It all got done much quicker than Thevar had expected. To him it felt as though it possessed its own momentum and was quite out of his hands.

The annual temple festival came and went, without Chidambaram there to enjoy all the fun and excitement of the goat sacrifice. 'He hasn't been able to get good workers – the right sort of fellows. That's why he's late,' thought Thevar to himself, and began to build walls for the huts he had constructed. That was not part of the original plan but with time to spare, he had taken it on.

Work continued at a brisk pace. When it was almost complete, an invitation arrived from the house of a prospective bridegroom for Thevar's granddaughter. This was the second time they had sent word. Kunjamma told him about it as he was having his meal.

'So! Then just tell me when we should leave!' he teased Kunjamma. 'Am I the seniormost person of this household, Mama!'

Thevar burst into laughter, almost choking. 'What does that have to do with it? You're the bride's mother! You are the one to decide!'

'I knew you would make fun of me like this, right from the beginning!' pouted Kunjamma, leaving in a huff.

'Come here, Paapa, little one[3]!'

'The little one is not here,' she retorted from inside.

'It's our big baby I'm calling out to!' he coaxed.

This brought her back. 'All right, tell me.'

'First bring water.'

'It's there in front of you,' she pointed.

'All right, all right! Now come here. On the way I saw Valluva Pandaram from the temple. Don't go on Friday, he

---

3   literally, 'little one', a term of endearment for a small girl. Kunjamma as the mother of a marriageable girl herself wants to be taken seriously, and spurns Thevar's patronising though affectionate way of giving her importance.

said, let it be Saturday, that's the best day. But I'll anyway go and ask our Iyer. If he says it's all right, let's go on Saturday.'

'All right, Mama.'

The priest responded favourably, and preparations were launched for the journey. Messages were sent to kinsfolk on the father's side. Ramasami Thevar from Vengoor and a venerable elderly akka from Meloor had already arrived in response to a special invitation from Kunjamma. The two elders filled the house with their gracious presence. And now the other relations were turning up, one by one....

All except Chidambaram.

Everybody waited eagerly for him. Till mid-afternoon on Friday he hadn't shown up. But a letter promising that he would arrive by Saturday morning had been delivered directly to Thevar's house.

A new kind of letter altogether, delivered into Thevar's very own hands. So far all letters for him had borne the following address:

'To be delivered into the hands of Saaya Vanam Puliyanthope Sambamurthi Iyer's Overseer, and the Headman of the aforementioned Village, Azhagu Thevar's son, Sri Sivanandi Thevar.'

When any such letter reached him, Sambamurthi would send a man to inform Sivanandi of it. And when Sivanandi appeared, he would read it out to him. Now Chidambaram had overturned this way of doing things.

As it lay in Thevar's hands, he felt his mind lurching back and forth until he finally consoled himself that 'Thambi' surely knew what he was doing.

His son read out the letter that night. Elaborately courteous and respectful in tone, its every sentence went straight to their hearts.

'Is it really Thambi who has written like this?' marvelled Kunjamma.

'This is not all! Thambi also knows English very well! Writes letters in English!'

Chidambaram's prestige and reputation had now received a further fillip.

He still had not turned up till sunset on Friday. At daybreak on Saturday they were to set off for the bridegroom's house. Everybody in the village had been informed, Thevar himself going from house to house personally inviting all the menfolk, and Kunjamma doing likewise with the women. Everything had been made ready for the journey. For the women alone, three bullock-carts stood ready and waiting.

Sometime before midnight, as he lay on the stone platform in the courtyard, Thevar heard a voice calling from the rear of the house. Getting up to take a look, he caught sight of Chidambaram standing there. In great excitement, he sprang forward and seized his hand.

'We have been waiting for you ever since we got the letter, thambi!'

'Had to run around a bit... Went to Kum'onam, then Thiruvaa'lur, then Naavapatnam[4]... Made a full round, Mama!'

'So...!'

'From Kum'onam twenty fellows have come. I've left them at the grove. I took a look at the huts you have built, Mama! What fine huts, Mama!'

Thevar pushed back his drooping whiskers and beamed.

'Please have your bath and come and eat, thambi. I'll just go and meet them all.'

'Where's the need to eat at this time? Let me also come with you!'

'All right then, just wait here, I'm just coming...' Thevar went inside and had them heat water for Chidambaram's bath. He got Kunjamma to rustle up a meal for the new arrivals. With the help of two servants, she undertook to prepare enough rice and sun-dried anchovy curry to last them till noon the next day.

'What you have done is just perfect, Mama! I was so worried because I was bringing so many fellows, so late at night, and wondered how I was going to manage with them, Mama.'

---

4   These are the names of three well-known towns Kumbakonam, Thiruvaarur, and Naagapattinam...as (mis) pronounced in the ordinary speech of the region.

'You thought this old man might have popped off and left you in the lurch – *posuk*! Like that! Eh, thambi?'

He felt suddenly humbled. They crossed the street of the Vellalas, and came to the bank of the Kaveri, and not a word passed his lips.

'Is Thambi upset?' Thevar said gently.

Chidambaram turned and met his eyes.

'How was it in all those towns, thambi?' asked Thevar.

'In Kum'onam one day I had a lot of trouble getting a meal, Mama!'

'It is a big town, no? That is why!' Until they reached the forest they talked about big towns – what made them so special, and so unfriendly as well.

It was still dark when they reached the forest. Peering closely at the workers gathered there, under their leader, the master carpenter Panchanatha Asari, Thevar surmised that in their hands the work would proceed satisfactorily. Of the twenty men, eight were skilled. For five years they had been working with the Asari, travelling with him to many towns and villages. The others were new men who had joined him only recently. Asari divulged all this as they went around the newly built huts.

'Mama, find out how much they want!' Chidambaram said to Thevar, on the way back.

'Asari will know, thambi. Let us leave it to him, that's the right thing to do... Here, Asari, whatever you say is all right with us. Just tell us how many cartloads of paddy you want, and Thambi will agree.'

'Paddy? Where do we have paddy, Mama? Let's settle it in cash – that will be much easier for us!'

But Panchanatha Asari refused to accept payment in cash.

'What can we do with cash, tell us! This is what a man down South tried to do – give us cash! I said to him, I can't eat cash, give me something I can eat! He made us run to him four or five times before he finally paid us in first-crop paddy.'

'The thing is, we don't have any paddy with us.'

'If you don't have any paddy with you, does it mean there is no paddy in the village, thambi? I have some paddy, and then there's Iyer and Chettiar too! We only have to ask them to send us ten cartloads, and they will do it. So why even talk about money, thambi?'

Chidambaram nodded, much relieved. But the exact wage had not been fixed when they returned home for their evening meal.

Work would begin at daybreak, come what may, and it would proceed at its own pace. Everything had been left to the team, so they could decide where to start and when to finish. This arrangement was greatly to Panchanatha Asari's satisfaction.

On his way to the bridegroom's house in the morning, Chidambaram cut across to the forest. Asari was pounding himself a morning chew of betel, areca and tobacco in a little mortar. He was very happy to see Chidambaram, and began at once to talk about the previous night's meal.

'Last night's food was very tasty! Wonderful garlic aroma, excellent nethili fish curry! Just like the karuvadu kuzhambu my own mother used to make! I wanted to eat two more mouthfuls! But where was the room? Stomach was full!'

Chidambaram smiled and said, 'That amma's cooking is like that – she has the golden touch.'

'Very true!'

They heard a rattle of bells, and cattle being goaded. Chidambaram listened intently. Then he said, 'If you feel you need anything, just send word up to the house. It'll all be sent. I have already told the lady.'

'Why bother with all that! I will manage. Is that our cart?'

'Yes, now I have to go.'

'Don't worry about anything, go and come back!'

'All right.'

Chidambaram crossed the Vettaru and circled past the Sivan Koil to Kuranguputhoor in search of Thevar. He found him under a mango tree, next to one of those hoary stone 'burden-bearers' set up by kings of old for wayfarers to set down their headloads. Lounging against that high stone bench and pounding himself a chew of betel and tobacco, he looked as though he were waiting just for him.

'Thambi's mind is set only on the factory now!' he teased.

Chidambaram laughed and sat down near him, leaning against the burden-bearer. 'Looks like the cart has gone the other way, Mama. You didn't get in?'

'I saw it coming along the edge of the field, and thought, let me wait for Thambi. So I just sat here.'

'I had gone somewhere... Got delayed, Mama.'

'Doesn't matter, thambi,' Thevar said, emptying the mashed betel-and-tobacco mixture into his mouth.

They walked along the tree-shaded road. It was a trip of two miles, and they talked all the way about sugarcane. How it grew, and how it came to maturity. After protracted discussion and with some hesitation, Thevar agreed to plant sugarcane on two of his velis. It was bottomland, by the riverside. Thevar had purchased it the previous year from Pakkiri Padaiyachi. Fertile soil, as good as gold, it yielded twenty to twenty-three measures per veli.

Chidambaram was greatly heartened by Thevar's readiness to go along with his ideas. Everything seemed to be falling into place. Of course it would take some time for the sugarcane to grow, and to be fit for the mill. Until then supplies would have to be brought from Villiyanoor in wagonloads. That would not be a problem in summer, but then there was the 'bad' season. The kaar-kaalam, when the rains would make it difficult to cross the Vettaru and the Kaveri. The waters would overflow and swirl around, and the carts would get stuck in the mud....

He began to earnestly consider building a bridge. There

was no bamboo left. It had all been burnt up. But that was no reason not to sit quiet. Bamboo had to be brought from somewhere, wherever it was.

Talking over these possibilities, they reached the bridegroom's house, where they were grandly received. Each of them was separately welcomed by everyone in the family. They vied with one another, jostling their way past to especially fuss over Chidambaram. He could hardly stand it.

Walking around the large house, Chidambaram noted everything – the inner quarters, the storeroom for grain and produce, and all the living space – just as Kunjamma had instructed him to before he left the house.

The would-be groom seemed modest enough, but he had a strange way of talking. To every question he would respond with just a movement of his head, or with a smile, or at the most with a single word. Was it just his nature, a harmless habit? Or was he trying to hide something about himself? To find out, Chidambaram praised him to many of those present. He also made fun of him.

The responses he received to these probings satisfied him.

On the way back, Thevar asked him what he thought.

'It's a very good match for our Paapa. Boy is as good as gold!' declared Chidambaram.

'A match only for Paapa? A boy can be a match for many women!' interrupted Velusami, who was walking behind them.

'Elei, just shut up, will you!' snapped Thevar, incensed.

But Velusami went on, 'Seerkazhi Anbu's son got married the first time to his maternal uncle's daughter. A child was born. Then what got into his head nobody knows, he deserted her and married her sister.'

'This fellow's drunk, thambi,' Thevar told Chidambaram. 'Doesn't know what he is talking!' He went on in a low voice, 'You know, this Velu – once he went with his wife to his mother-in-law's place. At night, the mother was wearing the daughter's sari. He thought it was his wife, and he...'

'What happened? Big ruckus, big fight! This Velu never went back there after that... Where's Velu?' Thevar turned and looked back. 'There he is, slumped to the ground behind us. Had a little too much to drink!'

Somebody went back to fetch Velu and bring him along, inebriated as he was.

The general opinion was that the prospective groom's family was very large. No fewer than forty plantain leaves were spread at mealtime. Indeed, it was like a wedding house, the crowd and the bustle. The groom was the third son; his two brothers were already married. The second had two children. The wife of the eldest had just conceived after nine years of marriage. The groom's three sisters were all married. The younger one was in Singapore. The other two had come with all their children to their natal home. Beside the father and the mother, there also was a paternal grandmother.

'Yes, it is a big household, but what does it matter? The sisters have been married off. Each is like a queen in her own house and family. They only come once in a while to their mother's house. And both the girls will treat her like their own sister! Our girl will have nothing to complain about in that household, anna,' piped up Thangapappu, a distant cousin of Thevar's who was the go-between. Also connected to the groom's family, she was putting in a strong word for the match, addressing Kunjamma's husband, who looked totally unconcerned as usual.

'How else will Thangapappu speak about her own sister's daughters?' said another cousin, sceptically.

'But I am not saying this just because I am related to them! Look, now tell me, this anna here, isn't he also related to me?' said Thangapappu, about Kunjamma's husband.

'Your anna is not even opening his mouth!' remarked Thevar ironically. 'He is the father of the girl, he is the one to ask, not me, I am an old fellow.'

Kunjamma approached her husband and pleaded, 'Please, look at me... we have to decide...'

Indifferent as always in all family matters, Thevar's son retorted, 'Why should I look at you in the daytime, di!'

'Ada wretched old fellow!' she muttered angrily under her breath.

By the time they reached the village, Thevar informed Thangapappu, 'I think Paapa will consent to this alliance.' It made the go-between very happy to think that her attempts to arrange the match had borne fruit. The news spread throughout both families. The wedding was to take place at the end of the month of Thai.

Detaching himself from his growing circle of relations and his newfound social obligations, Chidambaram plunged into his work. Clearing the forest was almost over now – they had removed the scattered logs and branches. What was left was a small area that had been totally charred. There wasn't much to do there. If they all worked on it together, it would all be done in just eight days.

'Come!' greeted Panchanatha Asari, when they reached the forest. 'Some good news of a wedding reached my ears!'

Politely but clearly ignoring the egregious familiarity, Chidambaram asked, 'How are you? Quite comfortable? How does this place suit you, our village?'

'Place is quite okay, nothing to complain about,' replied Asari, adding, 'The last time we went to work was in a place beyond Kolladam. Worked there for six months. That great man gave us a house to live in. 'House' means a really fine house! For eight births we can't forget it – my, what a house!'

'This house is just temporary, we just built it quickly out of urgency to get the work started. In a few more days we are going to build twenty stone houses!'

'So, then we can bring our family...' remarked one of the men who had accompanied him.

'What family? You mean your wife!'

Young Muragavelu tossed his head and laughed.

'This boy got married just one and half months ago,' explained Asari to Chidambaram and Thevar.

Thevar smoothed his whiskers back and rolled his eyes. 'I was also like that when I was young!' he boasted coyly. Laughter burst out, and claps! Those who had been standing some distance away flocked closer.

'Who's the man who wasn't crazy about women?' Thevar challenged. As they all gaped at him, he remarked, 'Any real man who's not a woman will be like that only! Like me!' before he walked away.

Going around the forest with Chidambaram, he counted all the trees left to be cut down. Panchanatha Asari asked Chidambaram, 'Are you going to plant casuarina here?'

'No, I'm going to set up a factory.'

'So everyone says.'

It would take some more days to convince them through his deeds that he meant what he said, thought Chidambaram to himself.

'Soon sugarcane and jaggery will be easily available here,' said Asari.

'But nobody can live by just chewing sugarcane!' said Thevar.

'That's one true word in a hundred!' said Asari heartily.

'We had to leave in a hurry, couldn't arrange anything for you. What are you going to do about meals, Asari?'

'Oh, nothing to worry! Thambi told just one word: 'Go and see the amma up at the house.' She gave us plenty of fine samba rice, and even found some pots and pans for us. Just like our own daughter, she has taken care of our every need.'

'She's just a girl…couldn't have done anything really properly.'

'No, no, mustn't say that, sir! Even before we asked, she gave us a whole set of pots and pans! But I forgot to ask for one more thing – a grinding stone. If it is possible…'

'I'll have it sent, Asari. Anything else you want?'

'Thanks to your grace, we have everything here!'

Panchanatha Asari's work went on apace. They sawed down the tamarinds, which stood there leafless, and hauled them away. On the southern side of the puliyanthope was the tree with the sweet tamarind which used to go to Chettiar's household – it was parched and barren now, blackened by the flames. They had stripped the leaves from three-fourths of the branches.

When Thangavelu arrived shouldering an axe to cut down the main trunk, Ramu was waiting for him. He stood leaning against the tree, his mouth full of betel, and greeted him with a nod. Whenever any tree fell against a house, or grew too close to a temple tower, it was always Thangavelu who went and cut it down. Hacking down huge chunks of it, he would hoist them on his sinewy shoulders and carry them away. When it came to work, he was a kind of hero, a champion. Nobody could come even close to him.

It was much the same when it came to eating. At every meal he would eat a three-quarter padi-measure of rice, unhurriedly, tasting every morsel. If there was some roasted karuvaadu, four extra fistfuls of rice would go in. Even before the rice, he had to down a pot of toddy – and a whole curried fowl. Having quietly eaten and drunk all this, without making the least song and dance about it, he would squat with his head down between his knees and fall asleep.

When anyone taunted him and kindled his temper, his lips would quiver, and his reddened eyes would flash about. He couldn't speak too clearly, for he had a stammer. 'Send your sister to me tonight!' was the only thing he knew how to say, and he would say it without the least inhibition. Everywhere he worked, he would get some woman or other. This earned him the envy of some and the hostility of others. He cared nothing for all that.

It had been eight years since he had begun to work. What went on in his mind was hard to grasp; equally difficult to pin down was his background. He never opened his mouth to talk about himself, or where he was from. A loner he certainly was, and yet a man given to extreme passions.

He was given to sudden erratic changes in behaviour. Climbing from a low branch to the topmost one, he would leap down to a third.

'Elei, Velu, you are going to fall, da!' Ramu would shout.

'Why are you bothered I'll die? Am I your sister's husband or what?' he would retort, with an unsightly grin. Then descending in two bounds, he would grab Ramu's cheeks in a rough caress. His virtues and vices were peculiar to himself. Often he would drink himself into senseless oblivion and get beaten up by the very woman who had invited him secretly to jump the fence into her house. Somehow these things did not detract from his reputation as a man to reckon with.

From the day he joined work he had not even taken a couple of days' sick leave. After working all day, he would sit by himself for a long while at night.

'Aren't you feeling all right, Velu?' Ramu would ask.

'Just okay.'

'I'll make some hot water. Have a bath and lie down.'

In the morning he would bathe in the river before anybody else, and sit smoking a cheroot.

'Why were you shouting all night?'

'I won't bow down before anything!'

'To a woman?'

'Elei, shut your mouth, da!' he would yell. And then, clasping his hand, he would lower his voice as though sharing a secret: 'There is something in that!'

All eyes fastened on him, he would expand on the subject: 'What is a woman, after all? At one spot along the bank a man scoops up water in both his hands and drinks it, and at another place, another man scoops up water in both hands and drinks it. Anywhere water is scooped up, the water tastes the same. Elei, Ramu! Do you see any difference?'

Ramu would not answer. This was a subject he disliked.

As Thangavelu ascended the tree, he called down, 'Owner's coming.'

'Right,' answered Ramu, and began to climb the tree himself.

Chidambaram was approaching in the distance, with two other men.

Chapter 14

AS THE DAY of the wedding drew closer, Kunjamma's duties kept adding up. For a while she was terribly nervous and confused. In such domestic and ritual matters it was Thevar who had kept her on course after the death of her mother-in-law. Whenever she was in doubt, he would gently suggest, 'Seems to me we can do it this way, Paapa!' But now he was simply not there to consult, immersed as he was, along with Chidambaram, in the business of planning for the sugar factory.

Soon enough, however, she rallied her spirits, and as she rose to the challenge of making arrangements for the wedding, she became more and more sure of herself. Occasionally at mealtime, her husband would venture to quiz her: 'So how is the work getting on? The wedding date has come so close!' With lowered eyes she would merely give him a long, steady look. He would gulp down his food, wash up and stride away with water still dripping from his hands.

He had his strange ways. Once he had eaten, there would be no sign of him until it was time for the next meal. He never took any interest in anything around him and wriggled easily out of any responsibility. When she was newly married, his quirks bewildered her. Then followed shock at the thought that her life had been ruined. She was furious at her parents for having got her into such a marriage. For three full years, she revenged herself on them by not showing up at her mother's house. Smouldering with misery, in her seventh month of pregnancy, she felt one day that she could not bear to live any longer.

'Athai! One of these days I'm just going to hang myself!' she cried, falling at the feet of the woman who had given birth to her husband.

Gathering her up in her arms, her mother-in-law sobbed, 'We'll be lost, Paapa! Don't leave us!'

Athai now began to care tenderly for her, treating her as though she were more than her own daughter. She became even more secure in the older woman's loving support and advice after the birth of her little girl. Life became easy. Her husband's behaviour wasn't so remarkable after all. She found that it couldn't put her down. She learned many things from her mother-in-law. Austerity, the disinclination to find fault, and a certain quality that you couldn't quite put your finger on...

If somebody turned up to ask, 'Akka, just lend me your gold chain, I need it for a wedding!' Athai would say, 'Why ask me? Ask Paapa, she is the person to ask in this house, I'm just nobody, really, thangachi.'

As for Kunjamma, she would exclaim, 'What is this, coming and asking me! Athai is there! She is the one who should give it.'

'This athai and her daughter-in-law are so clever... between them they'll sell off the town!' – That's what people said about them.

With the day of the wedding drawing closer, recollections of Athai kept crowding in. 'She was so strong, like a she-elephant! Got things done so fast! I should have done a lot more good deeds in my past life, then she would still be here now. If only I'd been as lucky...' thought Kunjamma, as she emerged from the inner room.

From the open courtyard came the rumbling of the stone flour-mill, as Kalyani rotated one stone above the other. To Kunjamma's great satisfaction, rice was being ground to a powder as smooth as gold-dust. There was something auspicious about the girl's hands, for sure; the flour felt perfect to the touch. Kalyani had been eight years old when she came to help out her mother, and now her whole life consisted of this one chore.

She stopped rotating the mill to ask, 'Akka, what should I give Ponnamma as wages this evening?'

'D'you have to ask me? Give her a padhakku measure of rice!'

'Akka talks just like her athai!' smiled Kalyani, even as she thought, A generous wage indeed...

'If *she* were here, I would have had nothing to worry about... But I'm not so lucky... I haven't done enough good deeds for that!' said Kunjamma, as she went to the doorway, thinking about the eight kalams of paddy to be pounded and husked, and the six marakkals to be ground to fine flour. The pujai at the Mariamman temple was on Friday, for which lamps had to be shaped from fresh rice-dough. From Ramasami Chettiar's, nine measures of whole green gram and black-eyed peas must be sent for, broken coarsely, and threshed for the offering of pongal. It was important to begin the wedding festivities auspiciously in the traditional manner.

At every sound of cattle-bells, she hurried to the door with barely suppressed excitement. Her sister Kokilam from Sittamalli, and her athai's daughter, her sister-in-law Sethu from Pattavatthi were both expected. Kokilam had sent word promising, 'I'll be there ten days earlier, and I'll bring Athaachi along.' Kunjamma thought she must have delayed Sethu. Hers was a big family, and she had four little children. Being the eldest daughter-in-law, Kokilam had plenty of responsibilities and couldn't leave all of a sudden. Sethu Athaachi wasn't like that: hers was a small, separate household, no entanglements, no harassment. It was just the two of them, and her husband was the kind who just didn't know how to speak a single harsh word. Any time she wanted she could have the bullocks harnessed and set off.

The carriage arrived as Kunjamma stood waiting, and Athaachi stepped down, her turmeric-washed face glowing bright. Overjoyed that both were now there to help her through the arrangements, Kunjamma rushed forward just as Kokilam stepped down from the carriage, carefully holding up the edge of her silk sari.

'Vaanga, athaachi!' Kunjamma welcomed Sethu, leading her by the hand and then turned towards her sister, smiling. 'Do you know how awful I felt that you two weren't with me?'

'It's all because of me, akka, Kokilam said. 'For four whole days I have been trying to set off, but there were so many things to be done one after another...'

The children jumped down from the carriage and ran past their aunt into the house. The bride-to-be came out of the inner room and hugged them.

'Come here, Paapa.' Sethu opened her arms wide and embraced the reluctant girl. Paapa felt unbearably shy. This embarrassment she felt she couldn't quite place it. It was a new experience, and she shrank from it.

'Our Paapa is already feeling shy!'

'Tomorrow she is a bride, no? That's why!' teased Sethu.

'Athai! Won't you keep quiet?'

'I won't!'
'I'll get angry.'
'So, get angry!'
'Then I won't talk!'
'To whom?'
'To you only!'
'You won't talk to me? Just look at me now!' Sethu lunged at her, but Paapa ran off.

Both Sethu and Kokilam took on many of the pre-wedding tasks without a second thought. For this was their own home. The wedding, the work that went with it – all of it was theirs to see to, to do, to see through.

Kunjamma, however, was needed to take decisions.

'Akka, just come here a bit,' called Kokilam from the back courtyard. She was measuring out the blackgram just brought in by Melakaram Annamalai Padaiyachi.

'What is it, Kokilam?'

'Couldn't you have said just one word, Akka? I would have brought this! Last year we got eight whole kalams of blackgram, more than ever before! It's just lying there!'

'You are with so many people. You have to answer to them for each and every thing. Last year we got three kalams in our fields, and then Chettiar asked for it for the wedding in their house and it was given away. This time there is nothing, not even for seed. Mama is running around with Thambi all the time chanting 'Sugar mill, sugar mill!''

Just then, Thevar sent for Kunjamma.

The long thinnai in the front verandah was crowded with seated visitors: Pujari Arumuga Padaiyachi from the temple, Kannayya Pillai from the riverside grove, Melakaram Saminatha Mudaliar, Neivilakku Samiyappa, the nadhaswaram player Uthirapaadi Pillai. On the smaller thinnai, partly hidden by the pillars, sat Chidambaram, and next to him, Thevar himself. At the sight of all of them, Kunjamma stopped just inside the threshold and called softly, 'Mama, would you please come here a little?'

Thevar went inside and asked her, 'Everyone has come. When shall we have the wedding tent put up?'

'We don't have many days left. Tell them to start quickly, Mama. Even tomorrow would be good. Afterwards, that annan will go off somewhere or other!'

'What are you saying, thangachi?' protested Chidambaram. I won't do anything like that!'

'Look, anna, this is a wedding!'

'It is as good as a wedding in our own house...'

Smiling modestly she came out on the thinnai to face them all. Kannayya began, 'So, the wedding pavilion will be in the centre, and we'll block off the north and east. I'll set this up just like the pandal we put up at Subbu Iyer's house last time ... Is that all right, thangachi?'

'It's a wedding in *our* house. No need to say more than that!' said Kunjamma firmly.

'This thangachi talks just like that athai!' he marvelled,

giving Thevar an appreciative look.

'You were the only one left to say that... and now you also have said this same thing!'

'For twelve years I have known Athai. I have come to this house a thousand times! I know her greatness. Now as I see Thangachi, I am reminded of her...'

She did not answer, but led Kannayya Pillai to the back of the house. Having listened to her suggestions for putting up an awning alongside the house, he remarked, 'It is only now I understand, thangachi... Why annan doesn't need to pay attention to all these matters in the house! You take care of everything!'

Kunjamma shook her head just a little, to stop him from talking about her husband.

'I will start the work tomorrow, Thangachi.'

'We don't have many days left.'

'Don't I know!'

On the way back to the front of the house, they met Thevar and Chidambaram coming towards them. 'So, have you asked what all has to be done?' he demanded of Kannayya.

'It is our family wedding, no? Nothing to worry!'

'Oho, such fine talk! And is that why you took so many days to turn up?'

'Eight days I was away...every day it got delayed...'

'Such an important workman! So the whole country needs you, keeps calling you, and all!'

'Anna keeps making fun all the time like this!' laughed Kannayya turning towards Chidambaram.

'So, then, I'll go and attend to other work,' Kunjamma murmured. Decorously lowering her head, she went back inside the house.

When she had left, Kannayya Pillai said in a low voice. I am not saying it just like that, annei our Sister-in-law has not died and gone away anywhere. She has fully entered Thangachi's mind. Thevar gave a nod, as though he were in perfect agreement.

As they reached the front thinnai, the chief mason turned up. He had finished building the huts, plastering them and laying the tiled roofs. Eight days from now would be the house-entering ceremony.

And two days later, the wedding.

In the matter of the house-entering ceremony, Chidambaram conducted himself in opposition to everybody's opinion. It would take place without benefit of pipe and priest. No sonorous drum, no Iyer to chant holy verses! This sort of thing was not to Thevar's liking, and he spoke of it obliquely. But Chidambaram was stubborn and stayed with his decision to eschew all ritual observances.

Leaning against the punnai tree in the courtyard, Kannayva Pillai the mason asked, 'After the wedding the work on the sugar mill will start, isn't it?'

'Definitely,' nodded Chidambaram, his eyes on Thevar.

'Do keep some stones and earth ready. The work will

go really fast then. We can build, finish, hand it over... all complete.'

'In two days I'll have a man fetch them here. Please come and take a look, and let me know if it is enough for the job.'

'I have set aside all other orders so as to do Thambi's job!' the mason reminded Chidambaram, and received the usual quiet smile in reply.

'I'll take your leave, now,' said the mason.

'I'm going to see Pichai. You are going that way, too, aren't you?'

'Yes.'

'Come, let's go together.'

A carriage drew up at the Ayyanar temple.

'Looks like our Iyer's carriage!'

'Yesterday he was going east, now it looks like he's returning...' Thevar was saying, as Sambamurthi's carriage came to a stop. As they all stepped back, 'Come, sami!' greeted Thevar.

'Your granddaughter's wedding, I heard...'

'Sami must come!'

'Me? How can I not come?'

Sambamurthi Iyer descended from the carriage, his glance falling on Chidambaram. 'House-building over?' he enquired.

Chidambaram beamed at him.

Iyer began to talk of the seasonal rains, and the pestilence that had struck the cattle. Kannayya Pillai suggested that a cattle-doctor should be fetched from out of town, and Iyer thought, too, that it would be the right thing to do. Chidambaram couldn't follow much of all this. He stayed silent, watching their lips move.

Getting into the carriage, Iyer paused a bit, then asked, 'Chidambaram, have you ever been to a Congress meeting?'

'No sir, not yet.'

'I haven't either. But apparently it is very amusing. They say many big leaders come, and that the speeches and the crowds are incredible. Once some big leaders passed this way... Thoothukkudi Chidambaram Pillai, Koorainadu Shanmuga Padaiyachi, Nagapattinam Abdul Kadar, Ettaiyapuram Subramania Bharati. We garlanded all of them!'

'Really?'

'That year, it seems the Congress meeting ended in a fight! I am thinking of attending the next one myself!'

'There is a lot of time for that yet, sir. Only two months ago, the Congress had their last meeting.'

'Seven months ago, in Kolkata, corrected Iyer. 'Such speeches! Such crowds! Neivilakku Ramasubramanian told us all about it, I could just go on listening all day long. And exactly what he said has appeared in the *Swadesamitran* paper...'

'He's a good speaker,' remarked Thevar.

'What is there for him to speak? What he saw over

there, he repeated over here, that is all!'

'That's also true.'

'Next time I am definitely going. Why don't you come along as well?'

'Certainly. Once when I was in Chennaipattinam, there was such a crowd on the beach! A Bengali called Bal – what a speech he gave! So forceful! I was really amazed!'

'Pal... Bipin Chandra Pal,' corrected Iyer. His name appears so often in the *Swadesamitran*.'

'I will look for it.'

'He is the star orator nowadays. Another one is Tilakar, from around Bombay...'

The driver of the carriage came up and whispered into Iyer's ear.

'Amma wants to know if we can move now, sir!'

'Oh! I forgot all about her waiting in the cart, I was so busy talking! So, Sivanandi, we will meet at the wedding. And Chidambaram, why don't you come over sometime, we can have a chat...' So saying, he got into the carriage.

'Then, I shall take your leave too,' the mason announced to Thevar and Chidambaram.

'Only your work remains to be done,' Chidambaram reminded him.

'Once this mason has given his word, he won't go back on it!' protested the mason with a touch of hurt pride.

'I am not saying anything about that, sir,' Chidambaram said, to placate him.

'Every man has just one tongue, after all!' declared the other, still quite stiff.

To this Chidambaram said nothing at all. After a pause, the other repeated, 'Then, I'll take your leave.'

'You must come to the wedding.'

'Definitely!'

They parted ways.

After the noon meal, Chidambaram set off with Thevar to look at the new house. Visible from a distance, it stood by itself, devoid of all the surrounding trees that he had chopped down. The deep-rooted jack tree at the back had been the last to be felled.

Opening the split-bamboo stile, they went into the open space. Narrowing his eyes, Thevar peered around. This desolate land had once been his garden. Teeming with sickle-shaped broad beans and cluster beans. Brinjals. Chillies. Yellow pumpkin and snake gourd. Three kinds of bittergourd: the usual paakal, the midhi-paakal creepers that grew underfoot, and the kombu-paakal vines hanging from supports. Those profuse clusters of vegetables seemed like a dream of long ago. Had they really grown on this earth?

The garden was no longer under his control – it was now another man's property. Even if he hadn't been the one to negotiate the deal and to sign the deed, it had gone from his hands into the hands of another. Who would now poke and prod and rake up the earth at his whim and pleasure, and he, Sivanandi Thevar, must not stick his head into it at all.

This was the first year that he had not planted the chillies and brinjals in their beds. As he had done for nineteen years every Karthigai month, he had sown the seeds, and the saplings had sprouted, but it troubled him very much that he couldn't transplant them. He was working with Chidambaram, Kunjamma was busy in the house. The poor saplings were choked and crowded together in the seedbed, and he didn't know what to do about it.

That was when Ramasami Padaiyachi came, asking, 'Are there any saplings?'

Thevar was overjoyed. 'Pull them out and take them all!' he declared.

Some escaped Ramasami's fingers. They had now grown and were yielding copiously, in dangling clusters. If all the sprouts had been transplanted properly, the whole garden would have been a profusion of brinjals and chillies.

'Come in, Mama,' invited Chidambaram, holding the door open. As Thevar climbed up the steps, his gaze was possessed by the house, which seemed to be quite complete in every respect. All that remained was for the house-entering ritual to take place.

Yes, the house had been completed. But it didn't seem as though the factory could be constructed and established half as easily. It might even take until after the months of Panguni and Chittirai. For a factory, an engine-room had to be built, a godown for storing sugar and jaggery, another godown for stacking the sugarcane, a room for doing the accounts, and another five or six for keeping materials and tools. That was all that would be needed, for the present. Afterwards, they could see what more was required.

A factory.

It also meant that those who worked in it would need housing. This was the problem with employing those who came in from other places. The houses that had been built now could be expanded and changed a little to accommodate up to nine families, but that would not be sufficient. Once the work began in earnest, this was something that had to be seriously addressed. If workmen were available, houses could certainly be constructed at a very fast pace. But where could they get workmen from?

The footpath connecting Saaya Vanam with the main road had been widened to allow carts to pass. This Chidambaram had done himself, along with Pazhaniyandi, because no other workers were available. Turn by turn they dug up earth and hauled it to build a mile-long road. It was a two-lane road, and two carts could pass each other on it.

Thevar was delighted to see it.

'Thambi thinks of new-new things each time!' he exclaimed.

'You see, Mama, many carts will be coming and going now. That's why I –' He stopped in mid-sentence, out of modesty.

'True, true, thambi!'

It was Chidambaram's new carriage that inaugurated the road on its trial run. It was a fine, dignified-looking spring-carriage, built according to ideas offered by Thevar himself. Everybody said it beat even the carriage of Rajam Iyer the landlord whose estate adjoined the jetty on the riverbank. The oxen, too, were a perfect match – tan-coloured Kangeyam bullocks with sweeping horns sharpened and adorned with little tassels by the cattle-man Pavadai Padaiyachi.

Malliyam Govardhana Chettiar hadn't been willing to sell the bullocks at first. Chidambaram had sent offer after offer, only to be spurned each time. It made him think. His carriage had style, and he couldn't harness blunt-horned creatures to it! He had to have those high-bred oxen of Chettiar's.

Taking a deep breath, he crossed the river practically in a single stride and went straight to Chettiar, who seemed to know exactly who he was. He asked lively questions about the sugar factory and the production of sugar, and was impressed with Chidambaram's careful replies.

'I've built a carriage, sir. Seems to me it'd be good if one of your bullocks could be yoked to it,' he said.

'Why not? You're welcome to drive it home!' said Chettiar heartily. He went to the cattle-shed himself and handed Chidambaram the rope of a frisky young steer who hadn't even got a full set of teeth yet. As he drove it along, he met Sambamurthi Iyer on the way. To Chidambaram, it looked as if he were just returning from Panchavarnam's.

'One of Govardhanan's cattle, Chidambaram?'

'Yes, sir.'

'So! You have melted him too!'

Chidambaram had nothing to say to that, of course.

Iyer went on: 'Govardhan is a stingy fellow – the cream of all misers! Won't give a thing to anybody! But when it comes to cattle he's got a real touch. If you get a bull from him, in a little while your shed will be full of cattle.'

'This is my first bull.'

'So what? One today, two tomorrow, then three, four...'

At the sight of the shed full of cattle, the young steer slipped loose from the halter and bounded away. Chidambaram ran after it and pulled it back.

Iyer watched him with a nonchalant smile.

That smile stirred his memory. Three years had passed, and so much had happened. Yet it remained unclouded and clear. What a strange woman! Even after giving birth to three children, her passion was unabated, and she could abandon herself. She, her drunkard husband and those children…

Instantly he strove to forget the whole lot of them.

When Chidambaram had first arrived from Singapore, Thevar had taken great interest in finding out how he felt about getting married. He had felt happy that he wasn't yet married, had searched for a suitable girl from among his own relatives. He even made some preliminary arrangements.

The matter reached Chidambaram's ears.

He extricated himself, saying with great respect, 'Not now, please, Mama!'

'Why? Is there anything special?'

'Nothing like that, Mama,' he had hedged, smiling.

But to Thevar that smile of his didn't seem natural.

'Can't understand what is in your mind, thambi.'

He did not answer, but sat there in silence for a little while before walking away. Even after this, Thevar brought up the subject of marriage whenever he got a chance, but Chidambaram didn't allow him any room to expand on it. He would just smile it away. Eventually Thevar wearied of it, and that kind of talk died down between them.

Locking the new house behind them, they came out on the street.

'So, where is Thambi off to now?'

'I'm thinking of going to the grove this evening.'

'Only after sunset, no?'

'Yes, Mama!'

'Then, please go now to the house and stay there awhile. Somebody or other will come, and there are no menfolk in the house. I'll just go and meet the flower-seller.'

'Right, Mama.'

Kunjamma was elated to see him and exclaimed, 'Without Thambi here to help, I had so much trouble!

Look, Thambi, how is this necklace?' She set the ornament in front of him.

He looked at it strangely, as though seeing such things for the first time. Kunjamma wanted him to tell her what he thought of every piece, she wanted to share her joy with him.

'It is very elegant!'

'Really?'

'Really!'

She took the necklace from his hand and went in.

Chidambaram climbed up to the thinnai and tried to lie down. But it was impossible. The loud and excited voices of women rent his ears. Shaking out his uppercloth, he threw it on his shoulder and was about to set off when Kunjamma arrived, asking, 'Where to, thambi?'

'Just to stretch my legs a bit...'

'Come back soon. People will be here shortly.'

He nodded and got off the thinnai.

The ten row houses stood by the bank of the Vettaru. Small, with coconut-thatch roofs, they were all identical. Four were occupied. Once the work began, more people would arrive. The engine driver would be there, and he would need a house to live in. Five more houses would have to be built soon, perhaps more.

In front of the third house, something like grain had been spread out to dry on the road, blocking it. Chidambaram bent to take a look. On closer scrutiny, it looked like some kind of insect, with whiskers and wings! He didn't know what to make of it. He summoned a boy who was watching over it and asked him what it was.

'Eesal, sir!'

Eesal! Winged white ants!

'What for?' demanded Chidambaram.

'For roasting and eating. With puffed rice and jaggery, sir.'

'Hmm!... Where did you catch them?'

'Yesterday it rained a little, no? Lit a lamp and caught 'em.'

'Are you Munusami's boy?'

'Yes, sir!'

'Where's your father?'

'Gone to work, sir!'

Chidambaram turned back and went towards the shop.

Plain goods like salt and chillies were sold in this shop. It belonged to Chidambaram but it was Thevar who had the whole management of it. Pazhaniyandi and Kokilam's elder son attended on customers. It did good business, things got sold at a brisk pace. People like Kanakasabai Chettiar, Parthasarathi Iyengar, Manavala Naidu, Patanjali Shastri, Vembu Padaiyachi and Kamba Ramayanam Murugaboopathi Pillai had all stopped patronising the old shop and turned to this one.

But now there was an uproar at the shopfront, and shrieking voices. It was not clear what was going on. Seeing

Chidambaram, a woman cried out, 'Owner's coming! Make way!'

The din died down as soon as he entered. In the sudden quiet the muttering of an old woman drew Chidambaram's attention. 'Come here, paati, what do you want?' he asked her.

'Just look here, Thambi, I've brought this padhakku of paddy. Measure it out and give me a bottle of kerosene, I told him, and this fellow says 'Bring cash, I won't take paddy here!"

'Just a moment, paati. One bottle of kerosene, did you say?'

As more and more workers joined him, it became difficult to pay them in paddy. At first he got enough paddy from Thevar, Kanakasabai Chettiar, and Sambamurthi to pay out as wages. But as the days passed, the quality of the paddy deteriorated. Wages were paid first in fine samba paddy harvested at Pongal, and then it was the rainfed kuruvai, then the reddish grain of the late monsoon, and after that the leftover last crop was measured out.

And then even that payment in low-quality paddy was stopped.

After thinking over it a great deal, Chidambaram paid wages in cash. There were problems, and much confusion. Counting it out, keeping an account – they had no idea of these things, and they suffered greatly on account of it. Neither Komutti Chettiar nor Abdul Kadar Ravuthar who ran shops in the village was willing to take cash. 'Bring paddy! We don't want any damned cash!' they shouted, and drove them back to Chidambaram.

Angry and miserable, they came back to him and threw the cash back. 'If you don't pay us in paddy from tomorrow we won't come to work!' they told him.

That very night he found a way out.

He opened a shop.

Thevar got Parthasarathi Iyengar to get him a little space in his second wife's compound. For paddy and for salt, prices were fixed. But in the early days they found it terribly difficult to count out the money, and to keep track of it. For many months they continued to regard money as a very troublesome thing indeed.

Taking the bottle of kerosene from Chidambaram, the old woman remarked, 'Thambi, if you hadn't turned up when you did, those boys would have driven me out. Tie up those rascals and give them a couple of good whacks!'

'All right, paati.'

Chidambaram glanced at Pazhani and smiled a little.

Chapter 15

THE WEDDING HOUSE had filled up with relatives crowding in from far and near. Face after new face showed up, folks with novel ways of carrying themselves. Women rustled around in many kinds of saris, their laughter resounding to the tinkling of bangles and anklets.

Thevar's house was swathed in wedding finery after many years. The canopied marquee was enormous, and took up the whole street. No cart or carriage could pass through. For the past two days, those bound for Madanam had to turn south and proceed by way of the street of the Vellaala farmers.

At the heart of that mammoth tent stood the wedding pavilion, festooned with bells and tinsel. A bower resembling a sacred mandapam in the midst of a temple tank, only more exquisite, it was hung with bells of various shapes, long and narrow, short and plump. Set in pendulous clusters of silken tassels, these red, yellow, green, and purple bells swayed elegantly in the breeze, their shifting colours and jingling chimes together creating a bewitching spectacle.

Around it careened groups of joyfully shrieking children. There were some little girls among them. Chidambaram stood watching their charmingly odd game. One tiny thing ran up from somewhere and hugged his legs, calling him 'Mama!'. Golden-skinned, with large darting eyes, she must have been around four years old. Ecstatically he gathered her up in his arms and kissed her on the cheek.

The child gazed at him, puzzled. Then, deciding that he was not her 'Mama', she slipped from his clasp and sprinted away. Chidambaram stood there, stock-still. A smile muffled in sadness appeared on his lips and faded away.

He went into the house. The courtyard at the back teemed with women. Men usually did not venture into this area. With bangles and anklets dangling from wrist and ankle, strange women were continually going in and out of the inner room, swooping down from time to time to gather up their infants. He stood there, his feet refusing to budge.

Pushing away the crowd, Kunjamma came bustling up to him. 'Vaanga, thambi!' she beamed.

'Where is Mama, akka?' he asked.

'He was saying something about having to go and

invite that family from Singapore, who came over by boat. He will come soon, thambi.'

'They've all arrived, it seems.'

'Yes, the groom's chariot should be soon here. You must go and receive them, thambi.'

'Without Mama?'

'Oh, Mama will join you later, he won't disappear anywhere!' she said, flashing him a sweet smile.

'So, this is Kaveri's son Shedhambaram?' cried an elderly lady, drawing near.

'Yes, Machi.'

Her gaze plunged right into him, her pallid face brightening with joy. 'What, pa! How are you? In good health...? You were barely two or three when I saw you last! After that, it's only now that I am seeing you again... That day, when Kaveri told me that she was leaving, she brought a padhakku of paddy for cash... When I gave her the money, she tied it into her waist-knot and cried and cried streams of tears...' The old lady grew breathless and had to lean against a pillar.

Chidambaram stared blankly at her.

'It's for her sake – for her good qualities, and for her grace – that you have come here! To show the whole family what she was like.'

He nodded, bereft of emotion. He could sense clearly enough that the sympathy spilling from this childhood playmate of his mother's came straight from the heart. But to receive it befittingly, and to express thanks for it, seemed beyond his power.

'You will be here for four days more, isn't it? I will come and see you later,' he managed to say, at last.

'You must, kannu! Just to look at you is like looking at my own son!'

He took his leave of her and walked away.

'Same features, same face... swings his arms just like her. Same way of talking also... It feels like she herself is standing before me, Kunjamma!'

'This is what Mama keeps saying too.'

'We were the same age...all of us,' the woman went on distractedly.

'Looks like Mama is here... I'll just be back.' Kunjamma went outside.

'They have all arrived, it seems, Paapa? Whom did you send to receive them?' demanded Thevar.

'Our Thambi, Mama!'

'Mmm...! No need to tell you what to do, is there!'

'Where is the chariot now, Mama?'

'Just on the way with the pipers and drummers right behind. Very soon the Thanjavur brass band will be here too, and we must leave.'

'Everything is ready, Mama!'

Reclining against a pillar, he enquired about arrangements for the dinner. She was quite certain that dinner should be served only after the groom had been properly received.

'That's all right,' mused Thevar. 'That is the custom, in any case. I was thinking it will get very late. But can we afford to think of all that? So...! We'll do it like that only, Paapa.'

Lamps glowed all over the house like celestial lights in the heavens. How many of them there were! In just a little while, it would be time to set off to welcome the groom. Each woman was getting ready to join the ritual procession, an unbroken tradition at every girl's wedding, firmly founded on certain beliefs. Ushering a girl from one golden cage into another was an occasion for celebration.

Felicitous sounds waft in from a distance. Along with the hair-raising thrill of the nadaswaram pipes resound the thunderclaps of Koorainaadu Pakkiriya Pillai's thavil drum. Flowers and sandalwood, rose-water and incense perfume the air.

A chariot draws up with four horses in harness. Silk uppercloth fluttering, the bridegroom descends before a temple set in the middle of the open ground used for cattle fairs. It is the Mandhai temple of the Lord of the Herds, Mandhaiyya. The Great Dark One, Periya Karuppu, is poised for the chase and strides forward with upraised sickle-arm, his great hunting hound at his heel. Golden chains dangle from his ankles and his neck. This is their own temple, with their own god, who rules over every aspect of their lives. It is he who presides over the spring festival of the sprouting of seeds, the mulaikkattu, and the annual temple festival with the lissome oyilaattam dance. Then follows the wedding season, with the solemnisation of marriages taking precedence over all other festivities, binding lives together and bestowing meaning on life itself.

The groom touches his fingers to the camphor flame, presses them to his eyes. He steps back to watch eight coconuts being dashed one by one upon the stone where blood sacrifices once took place. This is followed by the touching of camphor to that sacred site of sacrifice. On the eighteen steps of the shrine are trays laden with auspicious offerings. As the groom ascends the chariot once more and seats himself with befitting modesty, the women of his family take up the trays and walk behind.

The chariot rolls on into a black night dripping with bright lights. It embodies the remnant of a disappearing tradition. In the old days the groom always arrived on horseback. Well-combed and tufted, loins swathed in silk, neck garlanded, earlobes bejewelled, arms encircled with gold, and sporting a long sword hanging by his side, he would be taken in procession around the town. Every detail of his raiment and stance were in accordance with family tradition, based on firmly held beliefs. Mounted on a horse, the bride's maternal uncle rode up to meet the groom and escort him to the marriage pandal.

For every groom is Mandhaiyya, Periya Karuppu. God himself!

Women advanced slowly, swayingly, laughing and talking, their bangles jingling. They carried the scent of jasmine with them, and they bore large round brass and silver trays, some heaped with crystal sugar and sugar-candy, others piled with bananas, others with betel, areca and flowers, and still others stacked with saris and veshtis. And then there were large platters with mounds of the navadaniyangal, the nine auspicious grains.

When the procession reached the main street, Sivanandi Thevar instructed the groom's elder brother, 'Please ask the mapillai to offer archanai at the Siddhi Vinayaka temple.' The chariot halted.

The groom descended, devoutly circumambulated the elephant-headed god and prostrated on the ground in obeisance.

'Please, let it be done quickly!' Chidambaram bustled around, hurrying everyone up. For Kunjamma had sent word to him that the freshly-cooked rice wouldn't be soft and moist much longer, it was turning cold. One more street to cross before they reached the wedding house. Going north and turning south again, they would reach the Mariamman temple street and Thevar's house.

Raising the groom's lowered head, his second sister teasingly admonished, 'You aren't the bride! Sit up straight!'

He smiled shyly.

Stepping smartly up, the band musicians raised their tempo as the groom alighted from the chariot and was received with a tray of lamps. Someone waved the brass plate of arati, the auspicious vermilion water, in front of his face to ward off the evil eye.

'Come, come, everyone, please come... Everyone please come...' called many voices all at the same time, a veritable flood of sound interspersed with the rustling of silk saris and the jingling of heavy silver anklets.

The first rumble of drums came before dawn. The pandal was festooned with tinsel and garlanded with flowers. Yellow strings hung with bells in many colours crisscrossed the canopy. Fresh young plantain shoots pillared the little wedding pavilion. Facing it was the auspicious 'pot of plenty', filled with fine rice-grains, topped with a tufted coconut and fringed with freshly-picked mango leaves. Everything was ready for the ceremony: the freshly-fired earthenware pots and the freshly-sprouted nine grains. Then the grinding stone on which the bride's foot would be placed by the groom's own hands to the intoning of a benediction: 'May you always be as firm as a rock!' And the 'yoke', to drive home the lesson of obedience, the mortar and pestle, the bronze lamp dedicated to the Lord's beloved, the Lady Nachiyar. The mangalyam – the sacred taali thread with its two tigertooth-shaped gold pieces.

And on their separate salvers were the new wedding sari, the new veshti, and the ritual row of objects making up the bride's dowry.

'Bring the bridegroom, please!' commanded the

officiating priest, the Iyer, setting off sundry cries of Mapillai! Mapillai! Head downcast, the bridegroom walked up, clutching the hand of his best man, Kokilam's son. A mat woven from fine korai reeds was spread out for him over a layer of new paddy. Chanting the mantras and pouring quantities of ghee into the holy fire, the priest asked for the groom's new veshti. He blessed it with a sprinkling of nine auspicious grains, a muttering of verses, and a splash of water. Touching a spot of turmeric to the four corners of the veshti, he handed it, duly sanctified, to Sivanandi Thevar, who pressed it devoutly to his eyes and passed it on to Annamalai Thevar. All the assembled heads of Thevar clans and their wives blessed it likewise, before it was returned to the Iyer on its salver.

'Tell him to have a shave and take bath before he wears it.' Iyer instructed the best man as he handed it over. As he was being hurried away, the groom's brother's wife teased, 'What is the hurry? Escort him slowly, carefully!'

His friend hugged him close, practically lifting him off the ground, demanding, 'Like this, you mean?'

Waves of laughter swept through the crowd. A woman shrilled, 'Mmm...yes! Just like that!'

When the excitement and laughter had died down, the bride entered the pandal with her companion leading her by the hand. As she seated herself, her friend leaned solicitously over her to push a lock of hair from her brow. Lifting her chin, she ordered, 'Stay like this!' But Paapa's head sank down the moment she removed her hand.

The auspicious hour for tying the marriage thread had arrived. On a large silver salver lay the gorgeous checked silk sari, together with turmeric-and-vermilion, jasmine, comb and mirror. The priest handed it over to be passed around the hall, exhorting them to be quick about bestowing their blessings. Passed from hand to hand, the sari got stuck at one point. A detailed discussion was underway: every woman present was comparing the length and breadth of its glittering gold border with that on her own wedding sari.

The priest's eyes swept over the hall. He called out, 'You can admire it later! Bring it quickly, please!'

'Akka, give it, please, Iyer is in a hurry!'

'Just wait...!' The akka in question was still closely examining the bridal sari, unwilling to let go of it just yet. But Kokilam quickly grabbed back the salver and bore it off to the priest to be sprinkled with holy water.

The bride would not stretch out her hands for it, she was too shy. It was her companion who received it.

'Don't just stand there admiring the bride in her new sari! Bring her back quickly,' he urged.

As the music of thavil and nadhaswaram swelled in volume and intensity, Thevar was summoned into the inner rooms. Kunjamma was discussing arrangements for serving the wedding lunch. 'Have you gone and sat down to watch the wedding, Mama?' she said reproachfully.

'Chettiar has come!'

'So soon?' he exclaimed and swiftly strode back to the open front door to greet the visitor. 'Have you taken sandal paste?' He gestured towards the bowls of sandal paste, flowers and sugar crystals being offered at the entrance by the youngsters of his family.

'Yes, I've taken it, the boy offered me.'

'Only just now I had gone inside...' Thevar began apologetically.

'What does it matter...!'

'Seems Ambal has had a boy?'

'All three are boys!'

Thevar's grin disappeared into his mustachioes. 'Next year, your granddaughter will be born!'

Chettiar laughed boisterously. As they approached the pavilion he exclaimed, 'Looks like the bride has already taken her place?'

'Yes, yes.'

They went closer. Iyer was saying, in his great booming voice, 'Tomorrow she will lie on the same mat with him – so, nothing wrong in it if she sits close!'

A huge burst of laughter filled the hall.

'You said it right, sami!' shouted someone.

'Of course!' rejoined Iyer with a wide grin. These were levities that were unthinkable in any respectable agraharam wedding, but quite all right for these lusty Thevars, he thought.

Well within the auspicious hour, amidst the din of drums and pipes and echoing chants, as flowers and coloured grains of rice rained down, the bride lowered her head, and the taali ascended her neck.

All too soon, the bride was surrounded by women who wanted to bedeck her brow with pattams, gifts of gold medallions and talismans. Sornam tied the first one. As the eldest sister of the groom, she offered a whole pavun as pattam, with golden beads on either side each weighing a quarter pavun. The senior daughter-in-law of a large and notable family, it gave her great satisfaction to more than meet the requirements of convention with her lavish gift. Following her, her sister Rajathi, Paapa's second sister-in-law, tied her medallion on the bride's brow – a piece of gold weighing three quarters of a pavun.

In the old days the women would offer goats as well. Rajathi offered a silver rupee in place of a goat-kid. Only married women were entitled to offer these courtesies to the bride. Keenly disappointed at being left out, all that the groom's third sister, young Chellamma could do was to watch in wonder as each event took place. After women belonging to the inner family circle had finished presenting their gifts, the sisters-in-law once-removed came forward to tie their pattams. Paapa's forehead was crowded with gold coins, medallions, and beads, crisscrossed with turmeric-stained threads with betel leaves hanging from them. Oppressed and burdened, she tossed her head.

Her companion bent over her. 'It's over, just wait a bit, Paapa!' she whispered in her ear.

'Anybody else?' the priest called out.

'Please wait a little, sami,' said Aandal, coming forward with her yellow-threaded, quarter-pavun coin with a betel-leaf wrapped around it. And it went on like that for a long time, with somebody or other coming forward to tie one more pattam on Paapa's brow.

A crowd had collected at the entrance with the arrival of several worthies, from Kanakasabapati Chettiar, the Iyers and Iyengars from the brahmin quarter, the Pillais and Padaiyachis to Lakshmana Rao. Thevar's heart was full to bursting, he could hardly speak. It seemed to him that the entire world had gathered at his threshold. A glorious sight, it was almost too much for his eyes to take it in. At no wedding in his experience had all these great people gathered together. For these great people were by no means on friendly terms with one another. No two of them could stand each other, not one could bear to stand in another's shadow. Patanjali Shastri and Sambamurthi Iyer didn't get along, and between Annamalai Pillai and Murugaboopathi Pillai a supposedly lifelong feud had taken shape eight years ago which had been expected to last for the rest of their lives. No fewer than twenty-eight efforts had been made to mediate, and astrologers had been consulted to find out when the time for enmity would come to an end. All in vain.

But now both of them were here together. Everyone was here!

'We got here just in time, as the taali was being tied!' said Murugaboopathi Pillai.

'I am a very lucky man, I must have done some good deeds in my past life...!'

'Why so, Sivanandi?'

'Why not? Just like gods from heaven, all of you have come here!'

Not a word was spoken in answer. Instead a great tide of laughter swept over the assemblage and gradually subsided. All the brahmin guests, Subbu and Sambamurthi Iyer, Patanjali Shastri, the Iyengar who owned the jack orchard, and Lakshman Rao, sat side by side on a long wooden swing. On one end of another swing was Goverdhana Chettiar who placed his betel box between himself, while Anna and Ratnasami Pillai seated themselves at a respectable distance, with Uttiravadhi Padaiyachi and Arumuga Thevar next to them.

'Thambi, come and sit here,' they invited Chidambaram.

'That's all right,' he politely declined.

'What's there to do now, for you? Just come and sit, Thambi!'

'Sit, Chidambaram!' ordered Patanjali Shastri, before he obliged them.

'When is the factory going to come up?' cropped up a question.

'It looks like it will take a little longer, sir. Maybe after Chittirai and Vaikaasi.'

'It is completely new, this thing you are going to do here!'

Chidambaram grinned. 'Nothing so great, sir. Just a wish of mine to build something like what I have seen over there, abroad. If you all can help a little, it will come up a little more quickly, that's all...'

'Then, are you are saying to us, 'Plant sugarcane here!' Isn't that so?'

Murugaboopathi Pillai emitted a guffaw.

Chidambaram raised his head and gave them all a genuine trusting look.

Pillai went on: 'Four years ago in Kum'onam, just because somebody talked about it, Nagapattina Chettiar planted bananas in his brinjal garden. It all got wiped out!'

'Why go that far? Last season I had this desire to plant ten mango saplings in our backyard. What can I tell you? You will laugh at me! Not one survived!'

'Each earth has its own crops, nothing else will grow there!'

Chidambaram glanced at Thevar, his eyes narrowing. But Thevar sat quiet.

'Bride and groom are coming!' announced Karuppanna Thevar. Everyone rose, and with one voice welcomed the bridal couple with a hearty 'Vaanga!'

'Fall at Sami's feet!' instructed Thevar, and the bridegroom fell down in a full-length prostration, followed by Paapa, who performed a demure womanly namaskaram, crouching low.

'Dheerga sumangali bhava!' Bestowing a gift of cash along with betel leaf and areca nut and auspicious turmeric, Iyer pronounced a blessing on the newly married woman, which meant, 'May you always be a married woman! May you never suffer the misfortune and ignominy of widowhood and live happily with your husband till the end of your life!' Offering obeisance to elders and receiving gifts of cash was customary for the bridal couple. But when they neared Chidambaram to fall at his feet, he shrank back, saying, 'No, no!'

'Ada, what a fellow you are! Just stand still!' Murugaboopathi held him back. The groom fell at Chidambaram's feet, and received a smear of sacred ash on his brow as well as a pavun. To Paapa also he presented a pavun, and placed on her brow a crimson dot of kungumam along with the vibhuti.

When the bridal couple had withdrawn, Patanjali Shastri rose, followed by all the others who had shared the swing with him.

'So, Sivanandi, shall I take your leave?'

'You are leaving?' Kanakasabapati got up from his easy chair and joined Thevar in seeing them all off at the entrance.

As the carriage moved, Patanjali Shastri remarked to Subbu Iyer, 'The boy is very smart!'

'You mean Chidambaram, don't you?'

'Yes. He will come up very fast. Oy, do you know, he was the one who gave money to Ramasubramanian to attend the Calcutta Congress.'

'It reached my ears too.'

'Did you see how he gave one-one pavun each just for doing namaskaram to him?'

'He has a lot of money.'

'Seems he murdered an Englishman, grabbed his money, and brought it here.'

'Really!'

'Yes, really!'

'These Kallars are a robber caste. One of those 'criminal tribes'...'

'They'll do anything.'

Each of the wedding guests took leave of Thevar, and also separately of Chidambaram himself. He didn't comprehend exactly why so much respect and special courtesy was being extended to him.

The nine grains having been duly watered by the bride, she withdrew to prepare herself for the ceremonial entry into her marital home.

Chidambaram's mind was full of thoughts of the factory. He had not been at the site for four whole days. From the mason who had turned up for the wedding, he had come to know that the work had been almost completed. He must go and see it for himself. But just as he was setting off, Kunjamma announced, 'Thambi must come along with us.'

'Me?'

He had thought only married men and women, and venerable elders would attend this bridal house-entering.

Kunjamma gave a merry tinkling laugh.

Following the carriage of the bridal party was a wagonload of huge vessels as tall as a man's chest, with large salvers to match, brass marakkals full of paddy, many lamps, the 'pot of plenty' full of raw rice. There was also parboiled rice, twenty-one coconuts and twenty-one lumps of jaggery. All these gifts accompanied the bride, heart brimming over with happiness, to a house she had never set her eyes on before this day. From now on, that was to be her home, her house. It was there that she would experience all joys. And all sorrows.

One after the other, the carts turned the street corner.

Chapter 16

WHEN CHIDAMBARAM RETURNED to the grove after eight days, the construction of the engine room was almost complete, and the scaffolding had been taken down. A little distance away, a building was taking shape, and in four or five days it too would most likely be completed.

Standing in the shade of the half-constructed building, watching the progress of the work, Chidambaram saw Thevar in the distance, returning from the direction of Neivilakku. Having accompanied the wedding party, the old fox had taken a little detour and visited his mistress of many years, Sivabagyam! Chidambaram wanted very much to laugh, but controlled himself before he went forward to greet the old man.

The two of them went around, staring at the wholly transformed forest. What it had once been, it could never again become – the very grass had been scorched and blackened. The towering trees had toppled. Their roots had been gouged out and carted away.

The first lot of workmen had finished their job and left, except for two men who had chosen to stay back in Saaya Vanam. One was a mustachioed cart-driver, a burly giant of a man.

A murderer…

Before he arrived at Saaya Vanam, he had kept his own younger brother's wife for three years. One day, as he went happily whistling home after a bout at the toddy shop, he had spotted her chatting by the side of a haystack with a man who lived three houses away. For hours that night he had been in great spirits, laughing and carrying on in such a way that it really puzzled her. Finally she said, 'I'm feeling sleepy,' and lay down.

A shriek, and her breath came to an end. A curse, and he left the house. After that, his mind never suffered any perplexity. He imposed certain limits on himself, and he never once exceeded them. He used to tell his friend, a deaf-mute, that he was now extremely happy.

The deaf-mute Kumarasami kept two women himself. They were sisters. The elder one had left her husband for him, and it was she who arranged for Kumarasami to marry her own sister. But when the girl overstayed a visit which was supposed to be for just ten days and lingered on, the akka got furious, dragged her to the street and beat her up. For a whole month they fought every single day.

In the third month of her younger sister's pregnancy,

the akka's heart finally melted. She hugged her sister and shed copious tears. It looked as though the good fortune that had evaded her for eight years had descended on her little sister, and this cheered her up. She went to her husband, tore off the taali he had tied, and flung it in his face. Then she made Kumarasami tie a fresh taali around her sister's neck. As the years passed, the house filled up with children, the younger sister producing a baby every year, and the elder bringing them all up most lovingly.

The deaf-mute's household had come with him to Saaya Vanam.

One of his infants now ran past Thevar and Chidambaram as they walked towards the engine room. It was a newfangled building: nobody from those parts had seen anything like it. Built entirely according to Chidambaram's own design, it had turned out so exceptional that it had won the praise of a chief mason from Nellikkuppam. Surveying it, he had finally declared, 'You have done what we old fellows in the trade can't!'

They turned back towards the road. A woman sat weeping under a punnai tree, the same punnai from which the body of Lakshmi had recently been found hanging. There were so many stories about that death, Chidambaram had no idea which were true and which false. They were all sad. He had seen the girl a few times. Remarkably fair and tall, she must have been not more than seventeen or eighteen.

'That looks like the mother of the girl who hanged herself.' Chidambaram said.

Thevar looked up at him. 'Hanged herself? Or did they beat her to death and hang her up?'

'Is that the way it was!'

'Her older sister fell into bad ways, it seems. So they killed this girl.'

He shook his head, greatly distressed. 'This is very cruel, Mama.'

'Once my grandmother's younger sister laughed, and just because the landlord saw her laughing, her husband deserted her.'

'And then?'

'For a lady like her, it was a grave insult to her honour. Three days later she ground up some oleander seeds, mixed them with gingelly oil, drank it and died. …And then there was my mother's elder sister's daughter Chellam, brought up by the family with so much affection, true to her name. She was given in marriage to a brute who stabbed her and threw her into the Kolladam canal.'

'I feel so bad to hear all this, Mama.'

'If you really take a close look at this world, Thambi, it's like they say – split open a fig and see how many seeds of sadness are there within.'

'What you say is so true, Mama.'

Thevar smiled sadly. 'Do you know how much I myself have suffered?' The smile subsided, and his face was suddenly clouded by sorrow.

Chidambaram walked silently behind him, his mind in turmoil.

But what was this yearning he felt? Why was he so terribly agitated? Was it all wrong, the life he had led so far?

'What is that smell, Mama?' asked Chidambaram as they reached the road.

'That's Ramasami's cart, he's carrying karuvadu.'

'Such a terrible stench!'

'The fish hasn't been salted properly, maybe,' guessed Thevar. Chidambaram lifted up the edge of his vaitti and wiped his face with it.

Thevar suddenly said, 'Thambi, you must get married soon.'

'Please find a suitable girl, Mama!'

'Kunjamma has been nagging me about it for two whole months. For some reason or other I myself have been putting it off,' Thevar said apologetically.

But before Thevar could set off to find a bride for Chidambaram, the engine arrived. Enormous, with many large wheels, the very sight of it was intimidating. The driver from Nellikkuppam made his appearance only two days later. Slight of build, ebony-complexioned, and in a state of perpetual inebriation. A Christian, his name was David Saranathan.

Trying to unload the engine down from the large wagon

on which it was mounted, David Saranathan shifted it this way and that. Then he paused, hands in pockets, and just looked. With his restless eyes, he looked enterprising, decisive and very smart indeed.

At last, stuffing his nostrils full of snuff, he directed that the cart be driven right up to the new engine house. A ramp was constructed of long wooden logs, ropes were tied around the engine, and it was carefully brought down and hauled into the engine house.

And now that it was there, there was no need for so many men all shouting together. Now it was David Saranathan's job, and the job of his team of workers, to get the engine to function. He grasped the big gear-wheel and fondly kissed it. For him it was a wonderful creation, his baby.

The irony of it was that he had never loved his own children, neither hugged them nor carried them in his arms. Every time his wife conceived he would grumble angrily. All the infatuation hitherto would crumble, his speech and his behaviour would change so much he would seem like another man altogether. Every time, from the very same house where merriment and joy had overflowed, sobs and slaps would be heard. Pregnant with the eighth child, his wife was beaten by David Saranathan, and she died at his hands. He didn't shed a tear. He announced that he had been totally absolved of his sin by the Lord himself, out of the goodness of His heart.

At Nellikuppam, his whole life became bound up with churchgoing and working in factories. His passion for work intensified, and in a couple of years he had become a highly skilled worker.

Now he had come to Saaya Vanam.

Having downed two mud-pots of toddy and some meat-curry all by himself, he turned the engine's many wheels, oiled them, pulled the straps tight and spun them round again and again. The different-sized wheels began to move more and more rapidly and smoothly. Locking his hands behind his back, he strolled around the engine and looked it over. The engine was running well.

On Friday the sugar mill would start functioning. The priest had chosen the date and the time. Kunjamma performed archanais in Chidambaram's name at both the Mariamman and the Mandhaiyya temples.

It was Friday. A crowd had collected around the sugar mill. Many worthies from the entire region had arrived: Sambamurthi Iyer, Patanjali Shastri, Parthasarathi Iyengar, Kanakasabai Chettiar, Kuttalam Manikkam Chettiar, Melakaram Lakshmana Rao, Needoor Abdul Suleiman Ravuthar, Kadar Mogaideen Marakkaayar, Murugaboopathi Pillai, Uttirapadi Padaiyachi, 'Singapore boat' Annamalai Thevar, Ramu Thevar of Seerkazhi, Vellaichami Thevar from Kaveripattinam – the last two were distantly related to Chidambaram's mother.

Even old Subramania Iyer turned up, hobbling along.

Nobody had expected him, they were all utterly amazed. This person had once refused to bestow a blessing on him... but Chidambaram now went forward and welcomed him most humbly.

'Were you waiting for me?' quavered the old man.

Chidambaram smiled gently in reply.

The priest broke a coconut, lit a piece of camphor, and uttered holy verses to bless the engine. Subramania Iyer pronounced his own blessing on Chidambaram himself:

'May he become a wealthy lord, with crores of rupees!'

David Saranathan ceremoniously turned the key of the engine. As it chig-chigged away, its great gear-wheels crushing the stalks of sugarcane, the juice ran slowly through small pipes to fill a large vessel. It was pure cane-juice without a shred of fibre in it. The priest presented a silver bowlful to Chidambaram, who gestured to him to proffer it first to Subramania Iyer. The old man poured a drop down his throat and gave an approving nod.

That evening Chidambaram sent sugarcane juice to every single house in the village. To the houses of Sambamurthi Iyer, Patanjali Shastri, Parthasarathi Iyengar, and Kanakasabapati Chettiar, he went in person with his sugarcane juice.

Four days later, they made the first batch of brown jaggery, in moulds and balls. They made raw sugar too, of the type seen in Walajahpet up north. And finally they made white sugar.

Chidambaram directed the entire operation with calm deliberation. With a practiced eye, and standing at a distance, he could judge with aplomb whether the sugar syrup had reached the right consistency. Thevar couldn't get over his amazement and admiration at his intelligence and foresight.

'Nobody can beat Thambi in this world! Really, it is true, thambi!' he exclaimed. It embarrassed Chidambaram. Praise was pouring in from every quarter – from places where no one had even seen his face. Towns like Kumbakonam, Thanjavur, Mayavaram, Nagapattinam, Thiruvarur, where his jaggery and sugar had begun to sell extremely well.

The sugarcane that Thevar had planted on his own land sprang up fresh and green. It grew unusually fast, too, leading Thevar to remark, 'It is growing like this only for you, thambi!'

'It is all what I have learnt from you, Mama.'

'Adeiyappa... How you talk!' chortled Thevar as usual, clapping his hands.

'It is true, Mama! You may say it is not, but something that is true will never stop being true, isn't that so?'

'Thambi's heart is melting, just like jaggery!'

'After all, I'm a jaggery merchant now, am I not, Mama?'

'You are a factory owner!'

'Oh, is that so?'

'Of course!'

'Many more days must pass for that to really happen, Mama.'

'Days will pass, of course. Does time stand still?'

'You have an answer for everything, Mama. I can't win against you!'

'Me win against you?' mocked Thevar, laughing. Then he said, 'Never mind all that, thambi. Yesterday I saw Vembu Padaiyachi.'

'He said, 'What, annei, your sugarcane is doing so fine!' I told him, 'You also plant some, it will grow for you too.' Then he said, 'Chidambaram Thambi is also saying the same thing. This time the samba crop isn't doing well. Rats got in and spoilt everything, nothing is left!' Poor fellow looks like he is in great trouble. I told him to come and see you tomorrow, that you will help him. He'll come. Never mind profit and loss, thambi, give him a long rope.'

'All right, Mama!' When Vembu Padaiyachi turned up the next day, Chidambaram conducted himself with utmost generosity. 'I'll give you sugarcane seed and advance cash. If you need money to go and find workers, I'll give you that as well. But you must go on supplying sugarcane for the mill without any break – that's all I want.'

Vembu Padaiyachi nodded to everything. Taking the money, he declared, 'From now on, on my land it'll only be sugarcane!'

He didn't make good on his pledge for a whole month, though. Afterwards he planted sugarcane on a small bit of land – just a quarter kaani. It exasperated Chidambaram that he had been cheated.

He fenced in a stretch of common land – bottomland adjoining the river. Ten days passed and nobody said anything. He decided to pay a courtesy call to the village tax collector.

'So you have to fetch sugarcane all the way from Villiyanoor?' said the official, commiserating with him.

'Yes, it is very far. But what else to do?'

'Why not plant sugarcane here?'

'Who will plant it? My Mama has planted some. Vembu Padaiyachi has planted a little.'

'The others are afraid that it will not grow here.'

'Sugarcane grows so beautifully on my Mama's land!'

'I saw it. Adeiyappa! What a crop! Looks like my own evil eye will fall on it. Ever since I saw it, I very much want to plant sugarcane myself.'

'If you plant sugarcane, it will be very helpful for me.'

'I decided to do that right then! Three velis of bottomland, all sugarcane. How many times can you go on planting paddy? Let me change it once and see what happens.'

'With sugarcane there won't be so much of a loss.'

'Loss or gain – it all depends on how we ourselves do the arithmetic!'

'Very true!'

'How is the jaggery doing?'

'Not bad. Selling at a good price.'

'I sent our Alamelu a couple of pails of jaggery. She told me, 'It's very good! Where is this jaggery from? Send four more pails!'...Your jaggery has already made a name for itself!'

He grinned. 'I'll go at once and send you half a maund ... and of course I'll see to it that it is the best quality.'

'No hurry at all. You can take your time.'

'Your daughter wants it ... and what is jaggery if not for a child? I'll just turn one of the carts going to Kumbakonam this way a little.'

'Then why don't you just send it to Kuttalam itself? It's on the way.'

'To your daughter's place? Why not? Certainly.'

Chidambaram took leave of the tax collector and came out, feeling satisfied that everything was now in his favour. Returning via the sugarcane fields, he noticed that the young cane was growing well. Soon the sugarcane growing on Thevar's eight velis would be full-grown, tossing their tasselled blossoms like peacock plumes.

Everybody would follow the tax collector's example and plant sugarcane in their own fields. It would be sugarcane all over Saaya Vanam!

After the hot season the monsoon arrived. It was in the month of Aippasi, ten days before Deepavali, that the rains really took hold. They poured down in thick sheets without a break for two days and nights. The Kaveri rose above flood level and ran across the fields.

Both the cut canes and the sacks of sugar were stranded. The wagons could not ford the crisscrossing streams of the flooded river. In an effort of superhuman courage, Pazhaniyandi tried to ride the current, but the entire wagonload of sugarcane tipped over, and the flood bore him off. A mere boy, he was gone with the waters, and even his body could not be found.

In that black season of rains when nobody dares to build anything, when the waters had subsided a little, Chidambaram had an immense bridge constructed. It took enormous quantities of bamboos and timber. The bridge gave birth to a new energy and zest in the village. It was he who drove the first loaded cart across, steering it with great care, a great exultation in his heart at the thought that the problem of transportation was now finished with.

But no market was held in the village for three weeks, even after the rains. Men, women and children turned up at his shop to buy tamarind. Requests came in from Kanakasabapati Chettiar's and Melakaram Lakshman Rao's houses for their year's supply. The stock in hand was soon depleted.

He set off at once for Vaideeswaran Koil, Seerkazhi, Thiruvengadu and Kaveripattinam to arrange for supplies, returning three days later with three wagonloads. Of different varieties and grades, sweet and sour, all jumbled together. The careless pickers had even shaken down the unripe red fruit and mixed it with the rest. Cleaned, shelled, and de-seeded, only half the original quantity of tamarind remained.

The five pailfuls that he sent to Kanakasabapati Chettiar's house came back the very next day. Catching sight of him on the Kaveri bathing ghat, the Chettiar's lady called out, 'What pa, great man, doer of good deeds! But the tamarind you sent is not fit to put in the mouth!'

'I'll find some good puli to send to you, Aachi,' he promised.

'But you've burnt down all the trees! Where will you get puli now?' retorted Aachi. Turning away from him, Aachi squeezed out her silk sari, slung it over her shoulder, and slowly walked to the Pillaiyar temple.

Chidambaram stood and watched her go.

Unfurling like a growth in his brain was a memory of the puliyanthope of Saaya Vanam.

THE WRITING ON THE WALL
An Afterword

**How do we (sur)render unto Roman the
things that are Thamizh…?**

That any translation is primarily meant for one who doesn't know the language is obvious, which means that the work of rendering it in a different set of words and phrases in the target language is essential. But there are always some words that cannot and should not be rendered in another language than the original. Certain Tamil names, words and terms in this novel need to stand out and be counted as such, in their original forms, not just for the sake of accuracy but in fact because they enrich English, the language of translation. But how does one write them in a script that is different from the one in which they appear in the original work?

Writing Indian words in Roman script has proved to be a challenge for two or more centuries. Despite the tut-tutting of academics and purists, there has been a runaway romanisation, as languages respond to the inescapable challenge of contact with English with its idiosyncratic orthography. Yet the Indian languages have tenaciously held on to their distinctive sounds. Who wouldn't like to have a standardised, phonetically accurate and comprehensive Roman script for general use, one which eschews the priggish, daunting and keyboard-unfriendly diacritical marks behind which academics and scholars tend to barricade the already complex Indian languages? Should we follow the academics in the West who render Sa Kandasamy's name as Ca Kantacami (with a dash above the two 'a's and a squiggle under the two 'c's), or try for accuracy by putting an extra 'a' after Sa, and another extra 'a' in Kandasaamy? Some Indian words appear so commonly in English that changing them now would only cause confusion. They have become legitimate through sheer usage – such as 'Bharat', which gives the non-Indian reader no inkling of the differing lengths of the two 'a's. Or even 'Tamil' – which perhaps should be written as 'Thamizh' to approximate the rich palatal rolling sound unique to this language.

It is wishful thinking to dream of standardising and rationalising the existing use of Roman in thousands of Indian words, and particularly in proper names. It seems sensible to stick to accepted and recognisable usage but also not to flinch from rendering new words and names in a more rational Roman script. In doing so, it won't do to put too fine a point on phonetics at the expense of comprehensible communication, which is after all the first function of language. One has to trust that the approximately proper sound is being conveyed in speech.

Readers will tend to pronounce certain letters as in English, and it will turn out right. For instance, kurinja – where the final 'a' for the long vowel is omitted, for the simple reason that it is unnecessary.

I have therefore used established romanised forms in many cases, but have changed the romanisation of some words to get across the sounds of Tamil. For instance, I have used double vowels like 'aa' and 'oo' to indicate some elongated sounds. Ideally, a capital 'O' should be used for the word 'jOr', rather than 'jor,' or 'jore', and capitals for the retroflex sounds, such as R, N, and L. Such delectably Tamil words as jOr, oozhi kaatru (romanised better as 'zh' than as 'l'), puLi and kuRinja would only add to the flavourful *avial* of global English!

Take 'puLi', for instance, which means tamarind. I have preferred to keep the Tamil word when it occurs in conversation, because 'tamarind' carries nothing of the tart, tongue-smacking quality for which that condiment is renowned! Nor should one romanise it, really, as 'puli', because that word in Tamil means 'tiger'. Not exactly fit to be put in the mouth. Berating Chidambaram for having cut down the tamarind trees, the old woman says, 'The puli you sent is not fit to be put in the mouth!' But these ways in which the Roman script could be stretched to fit Tamil are not easily recognised yet.

Flexible and expressive, the Roman script is literally the writing on the wall for the world's languages. Better modes of romanisation are already underway as more and more speakers and writers of Indian languages lay out their linguistic riches before a globalising world. They need to be refined until the Roman script is freed from the capricious clutches and let-downs typical of English conventions of spelling. It tends to liberate Indian languages from their own ingenious and exquisite, but far too complex scripts – which were devised in ages when widespread literacy and multilingualism could not have been envisaged. Moving towards improved romanisation will mean that much of the thoughtless transliteration that has been taking place so far will be dropped. And that can only mean better communication in all the languages of the subcontinent.

Vasantha Surya

GLOSSARY

aachi: grandmother

aadathodai: Malabar nut or vasaka, a plant with medicinal uses

Aamaanga: 'Yes, sir'

aarti, aarati: a ritual of worship, in which a lighted lamp and incense are waved around an image in a circular movement

Ada!: an exclamation of surprise

Adadaa!: an exclamation of surprise

Adeiyappa!: expressive of amazement ('O, wow!')

Aippasi: mid October to mid November, a month in the Tamil calendar

Amma: mother, sometimes shortened to 'ma. It can be used to express familiarity or friendliness to a woman.

amudham: nectar, ambrosia

angavastram: a man's shoulder cloth. Unlike the thundu, or mel-thundu, this is an uppercaste garment, usually with an ornamental border

anna, annan: elder brother, also used to express affection and respect

annam: food, or a sacrificial offering of food to a deity, distributed to worshippers

Appa: father, sometimes shortened to 'pa'. It can be used to express familiarity or friendliness to a man.

archanai: a ritual offering to a deity, accompanied by chants and the ringing of a bell, with flowers, and fruit, a coconut, kumkum, betel leaves, etc.

Ayanaar: a guardian deity whose shrine or free-standing image is at the village border. A warrior with a sword, he is worshipped as a protector against diseases and evil spirits.

Ayyo!: an exclamation of alarm

chapatti-kalli: flat-leafed cactus with spines

Chellamma: a goddess of South India, with Dravidian origins, later worshipped as a manifestation of the Vedic goddesses Lakshmi or Parvati.

Chettiar: a mercantile caste

Chittirai: mid April to mid May

coolie: wage, or wage-labourer

dasi: sex worker, prostitute, literally the female form of 'dasa' which means 'slave'. In feudal society this was a class of women who were in hereditary bondage to wealthy landowners

di: a familiar form of addressing a girl or woman

erukku: a kind of milkweed. A large greenish shrub with ashy-white or pale purple flowers held sacred to Ganesha, with medicinal properties, it is used to treat scorpion bite.

Iluppai: mahua tree, valued for its flowers, fruit, and seeds

Iyer: a Saivite subcaste of Tamil Brahmins, sometimes bearing the name Shastri.

jaggery: unrefined sugar, brown in colour

jor: a colloquial term of relish meaning 'great', 'fantastic', or 'sexy'.

kaani: a unit of land, about 1.3 acres

kaarai: coarse grassy shrub with spines

kaar kalam: a month in the rainy season from mid-July to mid-August

kalam: unit of weight to measure grain, approximately twelve kilograms

kalasam: the crown of a temple spire, usually of spherical shape

kannu: dear, an affectionate term used for a child, or a girl.

Karthigai: a Tamil month between November and December

karuvaadu: dried fish

karuvaadu kuzhambu: dried fish gravy

korai: a grassy reed used for weaving mats

kudumi: a man's top-knot, tuft

Kum'onam: colloquial form of Kumbakonam, a town near Thanjavur

kurinja: a woody vine, ipeca. (gurmar in Hindi). Its leaves are used to treat diabetes.

Kuttalam: (Kutraalam), a town in Tirunelveli district famous for its waterfalls

kuzhambu: a thick gravy, curry

kuzhi: a unit of land, about 144 square feet

maa: a unit of land less than a kuzhi

Maasi: Tamil calendar month from mid Feb to mid March

mappillai: son-in-law. It can also be used to any man to show special respect and friendliness.

marakkaal: a grain measure, about 3 kg

mazhaiyum magapperum mahadevanukku thaan theriyum: a proverb *'Of rain, and of the birth of offspring only the Great God knows.'*

mirasidar: landowner and tax-collector

mulaikkattu: seed-sprouting fertility rite, performed often by women

naanal: a grassy bulrush, with white blooms

nadhaswaram: a wind instrument played on auspicious occasions

Namaskaranga: the Sanskrit 'namaskaaram', a term of greeting, with a shortened form of 'neenga', the respectful Tamil second person plural pronoun

Narada: a devotee of Vishnu, a musician and storyteller who often acts as a go-between in Hindu lore

Nayakars: a caste of farmer-artisans

Neivilakku: a town in southern Tamil Nadu

nettilingam: Indian mast-tree, a tall evergreen, also known as the false ashoka

nochi: a tall, bushy shrub with leaves used to treat lung ailments

oozhi-kaatru: whirlwind at aeon's end. In Hindu mythology at the end of Kali Yuga, the fourth aeon in the endlessly spinnning wheel of time (Krita Yuga, Treta Yuga, Dvapara Yuga, and Kali Yuga), Lord Vishnu incarnates himself as Kalki avataara to save the world.

oyilattam: a folk dance with sinuous movements

Paappaan (Parpanar): a colloquial pejorative term for Brahmin

paati: grandmother

padhakku: a grain measure, about 48kg

padi: a grain measure, about 750gms.

panchabhootham: the five elements water, earth, air, space, and fire spoken of in Indian knowledge systems

Panguni: Tamil month from mid March to mid April

pattam: an ornamental gift at a wedding, or a medal, emblem

pavun: from the English 'pound', or 'sovereign', a coin used to measure gold or silver

peepal: a common Indian tree, arasa maram (Tamil)

pichai: beggary

Pillaiyaar: Tamil name for Lord Ganesha, Ganapati

pirandai: a square-stalked cactus vine used in chutneys, and as a flavouring for sundried lentil crisps (appalaam, paapad in Hindi)

poovarasu: portia tree, with glossy leaves and yellow flowers

pujai: puja, worship

pungai: Indian beech

punnai: Indian laurel or oil nut tree, valued for its timber and for its medicinal properties.

saamiyaar: a mendicant holy man who has renounced worldly life

samba rice: a fine variety of rice

taali: marriage thread tied around the bride's neck by the groom, adorned with symbols of marriage.

taazham: pandanus screwpine (Hindi kewda), a fragrant waterside reed which women weave into their braids

Thai Poosam: a festival in honour of LordMurugan during the month of Thai (mid January to mid February)

thambi: younger brother, also used to express affection

thangachi: a young sister, used also to express affection towards a female child

thavil: a drum played on ceremonial occasions as an accompaniment to the nadhaswaram pipe.

thinnai: a stone or masonry bench jutting out from the outer wall of a house in the verandah, under the eaves, a sitting area common in Tamil houses

thumbai: a tiny grass with trumpet-like white blossoms sacred to Shiva

Trisanku: a mythical character cursed to hang forever between earth and heaven, often used as an allegory for one besieged by doubts

Vaanga, attaachi: 'Come, Auntie!' or 'Welcome, Aunt!'

Vaanga: 'Vaa' ('Come!' or 'Welcome!')' + 'nga' (second person plural showing respect)

Vaidheeswaran: (The Lord of Healing: one of the names of Siva) and Koil (temple) an eleventh century Chola temple

vaitti or veshti: a length of cloth tied around the waist and worn by a man, known as a dhoti in northern India. The former term is more common in Brahmin speech.

Vanakkanga: common Tamil greeting 'Vanakkam' along with a shortened form of the respectful second person plural pronoun 'neenga'

vanjira: seer fish

veli: a unit of land, 1.98 acres

vellaadu: a sheep

Vellalar: a landed agricultural caste

Vettaru: a river in Cuddalore district

OTHER BOOKS BY TAMIL LITERATURE IN TRANSLATION